Lydia knew **personally** *Lukas Gra* **the rules.**

But *not* getting involved with him would have been a waste. A waste no matter how this was all destined to end—tonight, or a week from tonight. That it *would* end she never questioned. What she questioned was whether or not it would affect her judgment or her performance as an FBI agent.

She told herself it wouldn't. That she was thinking as clearly as ever.

And what she thought—clearly—was that what was happening here was too intense for her not to explore. Being with Lukas made her aware that she needed more than work. It made her aware that there was another Lydia Wakefield, one who needed the touch of a man's hands.

A Lydia who had a woman's needs—needs that had not been met in a *very* long time....

Dear Reader,

The warm weather is upon us, and things are heating up to match here at Silhouette Intimate Moments. Candace Camp returns to A LITTLE TOWN IN TEXAS with *Smooth-Talking Texan*, featuring another of her fabulous Western heroes. Town sheriff Quinn Sutton is one irresistible guy—as attorney Lisa Mendoza is about to learn.

We're now halfway through ROMANCING THE CROWN, our suspenseful royal continuity. In Valerie Parv's *Royal Spy*, a courtship of convenience quickly becomes the real thing—but is either the commoner or the princess what they seem? Marie Ferrarella begins THE BACHELORS OF BLAIR MEMORIAL with *In Graywolf's Hands*, featuring a Native American doctor and the FBI agent who ends up falling for him. Linda Winstead Jones is back with *In Bed With Boone,* a thrillingly romantic kidnapping story—of course with a happy ending. Then go *Beneath the Silk* with author Wendy Rosnau, whose newest is sensuous and suspenseful, and completely enthralling. Finally, welcome brand-new author Catherine Mann. *Wedding at White Sands* is her first book, but we've already got more—including an exciting trilogy—lined up from this talented newcomer.

Enjoy all six of this month's offerings, then come back next month for even more excitement as Intimate Moments continues to present some of the best romance reading you'll find anywhere.

Leslie J. Wainger
Executive Senior Editor

Please address questions and book requests to:
Silhouette Reader Service
U.S.: 3010 Walden Ave., P.O. Box 1325, Buffalo, NY 14269
Canadian: P.O. Box 609, Fort Erie, Ont. L2A 5X3

In Graywolf's
Hands
MARIE
FERRARELLA

Silhouette®

INTIMATE MOMENTS™

Published by Silhouette Books

America's Publisher of Contemporary Romance

SILHOUETTE BOOKS

ISBN 0-373-27225-1

IN GRAYWOLF'S HANDS

Copyright © 2002 by Marie Rydzynski-Ferrarella

Books by Marie Ferrarella in Miniseries

MARIE FERRARELLA

earned a master's degree in Shakespearean comedy, and, perhaps as a result, her writing is distinguished by humor and natural dialogue. This RITA® Award-winning author's goal is to entertain and to make people laugh and feel good. She has written over one hundred books for Silhouette, some under the name Marie Nicole. Her romances are beloved by fans worldwide and have been translated into Spanish, Italian, German, Russian, Polish, Japanese and Korean.

To
Patricia Smith
and
fairy tales that come true

Chapter 1

He was going to live.

Jacob Lindstrom was going to live to see his first grandchild born. Maybe even his first great-grandchild, if the man played his cards right. All because he, Lukas Graywolf, the first in his family to graduate from college, let alone medical school, had decided to make cardiac surgery his field of expertise.

That, and because Jacob's wife had nagged him into taking a treadmill test, whose alarming results had sent the middle-aged corporate CEO to the operating table almost faster than he could blink an eye.

With excellent results.

Walking out of the alcove where friends and family were told to wait for news about the outcome of surgeries, Lukas let the door close behind him and took a deep breath. Never mind that it was basically re-cycled hospital air, it felt good, sweet, life-giving. And soon, Lukas thought, a hint of a smile finding its way to his lips and softening his chiseled features, Jacob Lindstrom would be able to say the same thing.

It was a good feeling to know that he had been instrumental in freeing another human from the grasp of death. His smile deepened ever so slightly as he turned down the long corridor.

This was probably the way his forefathers had felt. Those ancestors who, more than a handful of gener-ations ago, had relied on the knowledge of plants and spiritual power to heal the sick and injured. There had been more than one shaman found in his family tree and, if he were to believe his mother's stories, a few gifted ''seers'' and ''healers'' across the ocean in Ire-land, as well.

It was a heady legacy, indeed, he mused. Lukas was one-quarter Irish, three-quarters Navaho but right now he was four-quarters exhausted. It had been a taxing surgery, not without its complications.

Turning a corner, he entered the doctors' lounge. Shedding his scrubs, he put on his own clothes by rote, leaving behind his white lab coat. He was off duty, had technically been off duty for the past two hours. Except that Mr. Lindstrom's surgery hadn't ex-actly gone as planned. They'd almost lost the man twice.

Lindstrom's vital signs were good now and there was every chance for a strong, rapid recovery.

Lukas had said as much to the man's wife and grown children, who had spent the last few hours contemplating the possible demise of a man they had heretofore regarded as indestructible. He had barely finished talking when Mrs. Lindstrom had hugged him and blessed him.

He wasn't much for physical contact, but he knew the woman needed it so he had stood still and allowed himself to be embraced, had even patted her on the shoulder. He'd left the woman with tears of joy in her eyes, counting the minutes until she could see her husband again.

Lukas's mouth curved a little more as he shut his locker door. This was why he'd become a surgeon in the first place, why he had set his sights on heart surgery. The heart was the center of everything within a human being.

His goal was simple: to heal and preserve as many lives as he could. He figured the reason he'd been put on earth was to make a difference and he intended to do just that.

The rush that came over him was incredible and he paused beside the locker for a moment to savor it. He was one of the lucky ones, he knew. He could still feel the overwhelming elation after each surgery that went well. There were many in the medical community who had burned out, who performed surgery by the numbers and felt none of the gratification that he was feeling now.

They didn't know what they were missing, Lukas

thought, pity wafting through him. He picked up his windbreaker, feeling as if he could pretty near walk on water. Or at the very least, on some very deep puddles.

As he started to open the door to leave, it swung open. Allan Pierce, a first-year intern, stumbled in on the long end of a thirty-six-hour shift. His eyes brightened slightly, the way a private's did in the presence of a four-star general.

"You on duty tonight, Dr. Graywolf?"

"Off," Lukas told him crisply.

He could already visualize his bed, visualize his body sprawled out on top of it, the comforter lying in a crumpled heap on one or the other side of his body. Though it was only a year in his past, he'd gotten completely out of the habit of the long hours that interning and residency demanded. It wasn't something he cared to revisit on a regular basis.

"Wish I were," Allan mumbled. His shaggy blond hair drooped into his eyes, making him seem years younger than he was.

"You will be," Lukas promised, feeling uncustomarily lighthearted. As a rule, he was distant with the interns. "In about five years. 'Night."

So saying, Lukas walked out of the lounge and directly into the path of turmoil.

The rear doors of the emergency room sprang open as two ambulance attendants rushed in. A gust of leaves, chasing one another in the late autumn wind, swirled around the wheels of the gurney. The wounded man strapped to its board was screaming obscenities at anyone within earshot, but most were directed at the slender, no-nonsense blonde keeping pace with the attendants.

For just a second, as the wind lifted the edge of her jacket, Lukas thought he saw the hilt of a revolver. But then her jacket fell closed again and he found himself wondering if he'd just imagined the weapon.

Another man, older than the woman by at least a decade and wearing a three-piece suit, followed slightly behind her.

The man looked winded as he vainly attempted to catch up to the woman. Carrying a little too much weight for his age and height, Lukas judged. He wondered when the man had last had a treadmill test.

But there was little time for extraneous thoughts. The noise level and tension rose with each passing second. Nurses and attendants began to converge around the incoming gurney. From where he stood, Lukas had a clear view. He could see all the blood the man had lost. And the handcuffs that tethered him to the gurney.

One of the attendants was rattling off vital signs to the nearest nurse while the blonde interrupted with orders of her own. The screaming man on the gurney was a gunshot victim.

And then suddenly the patient fell eerily silent, pale in his stillness. He sank back against the gurney.

Lukas lost no time cutting the distance between

himself and the injured man, pushing his way into the center of what looked as if it could easily become a mob scene.

Out of the corner of his eye, he saw the blonde frown at him. Placing his fingers on the artery in the man's neck, he found no pulse.

The blonde grabbed his arm. "Who are you?" she demanded.

Lukas saw no reason to waste time answering her. There was a life at stake.

"Crash cart," he ordered the closest nurse to him. "Now!" The dark-haired woman quickly disappeared into the crowd.

"Is he dead?" The blonde wanted to know. When Lukas didn't say anything, she moved so that he was forced to look at her. Her hand gripped his wrist, her intent clear. She was going to hold it still until she got her answer. The strength he felt there didn't surprise him. "Is he dead?" she repeated.

"Not yet," Lukas snapped, jerking his wrist away.

The nurse he'd sent for the crash cart returned, hurrying to position it next to the gurney. There was no time to get the man to a room. What had to be done was going to be done in the corridor, with everyone looking on.

"Someone get his shirt open!" Lukas ordered.

He was surprised when the blonde was the first to comply, ripping the man's shirt down the center. He saw the blood on her hands and arm then. Lukas pushed the questions back as he held the paddles up to have the lubricant applied. Directing the amount of voltage to be used, he held the paddles ready as he announced the customary, "Clear." At the last second he jerked back the paddles when he saw that the blonde had one hand on the victim.

What was she doing, playing games? "Clear!" Lukas shouted at her angrily. "That means get your hands away from the patient unless you want to feel the roots of your hair stand on end."

Glaring at him, the blonde elaborately raised both her hands up and away from the man on the gurney.

The monitor continued to display a flat line as Lukas tried once and then again to bring the man around. Raising the voltage, Lukas tried a third time and was rewarded with a faint blip on the screen.

He held his breath as he watched the monitor. The blip grew stronger. Lukas began to breathe again. He replaced the paddles on the cart.

"Get him to Room Twelve," he instructed Pierce, who had been hovering at his elbow the entire time.

"Right away."

Lukas took another deep breath as his adrenaline began to level off. From the looks of it, his night had just gotten a whole lot longer. By the time they could get another heart specialist down to the hospital, it might be too late for the man they'd just brought in. Casting no aspersions on the doctor on duty, Lukas knew he was better at this sort of thing than Carlucci was.

As with every patient he came in contact with, he

felt responsible. He blamed it in part on his grandmother's stories about the endless circle of life, how
each person touched another. Was responsible for another. Between his grandmother and the Hippocratic
oath, there wasn't much margin for indifference.

He paused only long enough to wash his hands and
slip on the disposable yellow gown the nurse—who
seemed to materialize from out of nowhere—was
holding up for him. The surgical gloves slid on like
a second skin. They very nearly were.

Entering Room Twelve, Lukas nodded at Harrison
MacKenzie, surprised to see the man there. He must
have been in the area when he heard about the gunshot victim. Following the light in Harrison's eyes,
Lukas became aware of the woman again. She was
shadowing his every move. Or rather, the man on the
gurney's every move.

Lukas spared her a glare as the paramedics and
attendings transferred the patient onto the examination table. "You're not supposed to be here."

The blonde didn't budge a fraction of an inch. Even
as the gurney was being removed. They went around
her. "He's here, I'm here."

Lukas assessed the damage quickly. There was a
bullet lodged dangerously close to the man's heart.
"I take it that it's not filial loyalty that's keeping you
in my way."

The term almost made her choke. Her eyes glinted
with loathing, the kind displayed for a creature that
was many levels beneath human and dangerous.

"He and his friends just tried to blow up most of the Crossways Mall," the blonde informed him grimly. "His friends got away. I'm not letting this one out of my sight."

"The windows aren't made of lead." His hands full, Lukas nodded toward the swinging doors. "You can keep him in your sight from the hallway." The fact that she remained standing where she was threatened to unravel the temper he usually kept securely under wraps. "The man's losing blood at a rate that could shortly kill him, he's shackled to a bed and he's unconscious. Take it from me, he's not going anywhere in the next hour. Maybe two. Now I'm not going to tell you again. Get outside."

Frustrated, Special Agent Lydia Wakefield spun on her heel. The flat of her hand slapped against the swinging door as she pushed it open and stormed out of the room. The older man who had come in with her followed silently in her shadow.

"I'd say someone needs to work on their people skills," Harrison observed.

Lukas looked up at the man who had befriended him in medical school, the man he felt closer to than anyone, other than his uncle Henry. There was a mask covering his face, but Lukas could feel the other man's grin. "You talking about me, or her?"

The smile reached Harrison's blue eyes, crinkling them. "A little of both." He looked down at the patient. "I heard the commotion all the way to the elevator. I thought I'd offer you an extra set of hands, but it doesn't look like you'll be needing me."

Harrison's field of expertise was plastic surgery. He specialized in trauma victims.

If he knew Harry, the man probably had a hot date stashed somewhere. There was no need to keep him from her. Lukas shook his head. "Not unless he intends to wear his heart on his sleeve."

Harrison remained a few minutes longer, just in case. "Did I hear her right?" He nodded at the man on the table. "You operating on a bomber?"

"I'm operating on a man," Lukas corrected. "Whatever else he is is between him and his god. I'm not here to play judge and jury. I just patch up bodies."

Harrison stepped back, undoing his mask. Drooping, it hung around his neck. "Well, I see that, as usual, you're keeping things light." He looked at his watch. If he bent a few speeding rules, he could still make his date on time. "I've got cold champagne and a hot woman waiting for me, so I'll just leave you to your jigsaw puzzle." Shedding the yellow paper gown, he tossed it into the bin in the corner.

Walking out, Harrison stopped to talk to the blonde, who was standing inches away from the swinging door. He had a weakness for determined women.

"Don't worry, he's as good as they make 'em," he assured her.

She frowned. Right now, she wasn't all that concerned about tapping into miracles to prolong the life of a man she considered pure scum.

"Just means the taxpayers are going to have to spend more money," she said without looking at the doctor at her side.

"Come again?"

Standing at the window, she watched as people ran back and forth, getting what looked to be units of blood, doing things she wasn't even vaguely familiar with. "If your friend saves his life, there's going to be a lengthy trial."

Harrison glanced at the man who had come in with the blonde before looking back at her. "Everybody deserves his day in court."

She had thought that once, too. Before the job had gotten to her. Before she'd seen what she had today. She turned from the window to glare at the doctor spouting ideologies.

Her eyes were cold. "A man who would blow up innocent people to vent his anger or to carry out some kind of private war doesn't deserve anything."

Harrison took quiet measure of her. The woman appeared to be a handful by anyone's standards. Probably gave her superiors grief. Not unlike Lukas on a good day, he mused.

"Odd philosophy for a law enforcement agent."

"Oh, really?" Tired and in no mood for pretty-boy doctors who probably saw themselves as several cuts above the average man and only slightly below God, she fisted her hand at her waist. "And what makes you such an expert on law enforcement agents?"

"I'm not," Harrison said. A seductive smile spread along his lips as he regarded her. "But give me time and I could be."

Lydia saw her partner move closer and held up her hand to stop him in his place. "I think you'd better go now."

Harrison raised his hands in complete surrender, taking one step back, and then another. He had places to be, anyway. With a woman who was perhaps not as exciting as this one, but who, he was willing to bet, was a whole lot more accommodating.

"Okay, but go easy on my friend." He nodded toward the room he'd just vacated. "His head doesn't grow back if you rip it off."

She glared at the doctor's back as he walked quickly away. It was easy to be flippant, to espouse mercy and understanding if you were ignorant of the circumstances. If you hadn't just seen a teenage boy destroyed, a life that was far too short snuffed out right before your eyes.

Restless, Lydia couldn't settle down, couldn't keep from moving. If only she and Elliot had gotten there earlier.

But the tip they'd received had been too late. It had sent them to Conroy's house, where they had uncovered enough powder and detonating devices to blow up half the state. It was by chance that they'd stumbled across the intended target: the Crossroads Mall exhibit honoring Native American history.

They'd rushed to the Crossroads, calling in local police, calling ahead to the mall's security guards. To no avail. She couldn't stop the bombing, couldn't get the mall evacuated in time. She tried to console herself with the fact that things could have been worse. If this had happened at an earlier hour, the damage would have been far greater in terms of lives lost. And fortunately, it had happened in the middle of the week, which didn't see as much foot traffic at the mall as a Friday or Saturday night.

The bombing, according to a note sent to the local news station and received within the past hour, had been meant as a warning.

For Lydia, even one life lost because of some crazed supremacy group's idea of justice was one too many. And there had been a life lost. Not to mention the number of people injured and maimed. The ambulances had arrived en masse, and the victims being taken to three trauma hospitals in the area.

Knowing that only Blair Memorial had an area set aside for prisoners, so the paramedics had brought them here.

And now the doctor with the solemn face and gaunt, high cheekbones was trying to save the life of a man who had no regard for other lives.

It was a hell of a strange world she lived in.

Lydia leaned her forehead against the glass, absorbing the coolness, wishing her headache would go away.

"I can take it from here, Lyd," Elliot was saying behind her. "You're beat. Why don't you go home, get some rest?"

She turned to the man who had been her partner from the first day she'd walked into the Santa Ana FBI building. At the time she'd felt she was being adopted rather than partnered. Elliot Peterson looked more like someone who should be behind a counter, selling toys, not a man who regularly went to target practice and had two guns strapped to his body for most of each day. He was ten years older than her, and acted as if he were double that. Elliot took on the role of the father she'd lost more than a dozen years ago. At times, that got in the way.

He was always trying to make her job easier.

Lydia smiled as she shook her head. She wasn't about to go anywhere. "You're the one with a wife and kids waiting for you. All I've got waiting for me is a television set."

"And whose fault is that?" It was no secret that he and his wife had tried to play matchmaker for her, to no avail. Loose, wide shoulders lifted in a half shrug. There was no denying that he wanted to get home himself.

"Yeah, but…"

There was no need for both of them to remain here. "How long since you and Janice had some quality time together?"

Elliot pretended to consider the question. "Does the birthing room at the hospital count?"

Lydia laughed. "No."

"Then I don't remember."

She looked at him knowingly. "That's what I thought. Go home, Elliot. Kiss your wife and hug your kids and tell them all to stay out of malls for a while."

The warning hit too close to home. His oldest daughter, Jamie, liked to hang out with her friends at the Crossroads on weekends. If this had been Saturday morning instead of Wednesday night...

He didn't want to go there. Suddenly ten paces beyond weary, Elliot decided to take Lydia up on her offer. "You sure?"

This job could easily be turned over to someone in a lower position for now, but she wouldn't feel right about leaving until she knew what condition the bomber was in.

She started to gesture toward the closed doors behind her. Pain shot through her arm and she carefully lowered it, hoping Elliot hadn't noticed. He could fuss more than a mother hen once he got going.

She nodded toward the room. "As the good doctor pointed out, that guy's not going anywhere tonight. I can handle it from here. If anything breaks, I can always page you."

Grateful for the reprieve, Elliot patted her shoulder. "Night or day." He glanced through the window. The medical team was still going full steam. "From the looks of it, it might be a while. Want me to get you some coffee before I go, maybe find you something clean to put on?''

She glanced down at her bloodied jacket. ''My dry cleaner is not going to be happy about this. And, thanks, but I'll find the coffee myself.'' She didn't like to be waited on. Besides, Elliot had put in just as full a day as she had. ''You just go home to Janice before she starts thinking I have designs on you.''

Looking back at his life, he sometimes thought he'd been born married. Janice had been his first sweetheart in junior high. ''Not a chance. Janice knows there isn't an unfaithful bone in my body.''

That makes you one of the rare ones, Elliot, Lydia thought as she watched her partner walk down the long corridor. She vaguely wondered if there would ever be someone like that in her life, then dismissed the thought. She was married to her job, which was just the way she wanted it. No one to worry about her and no one to worry about when she put herself on the line. Clean and neat. She was too busy to be lonely.

''You'd think a state-of-the-art hospital would keep coffee machines in plain sight,'' she muttered to herself, looking up and down the corridor. About to approach the receptionist at the emergency admissions desk, she heard the doors behind her swoosh open.

Turning, she saw the doctor who had earlier hustled her out of Room Twelve hurrying alongside an unconscious, gurneyed Conroy. They had transferred the suspect back onto a gurney and he was being wheeled out.

She lost no time falling in beside the doctor. "Is he stable?" she asked. "Can I question him?"

Stopping at the service elevator, Lukas pressed the up button. He'd never cared for authority, had found it daunting and confining as a teenager. The run-ins he had had with the law before his uncle had taken him under his wing and straightened him out had left a bad taste in his mouth.

"You can if you don't want any answers." The elevator doors opened. The orderly with him pushed the gurney inside and Lukas took his place beside it. "He needs immediate surgery, not a game of Twenty Questions."

"What floor?" she demanded as the doors began to close.

Lukas pretended to cock his head as if he hadn't heard her. "What?"

Irritated, she raised her voice. "What floor are you taking him to?"

The doors closed before he gave her an answer. Not that he looked as if he was going to, she thought angrily. What was his problem? Did he have an affinity for men who tried to blow up young girls and cut down young boys for sport because of some half-baked ideas about supremacy?

Her temper on the verge of a major explosion, Lydia hurried back to the emergency room admissions desk and cornered the clerk before he could get away.

"That tall, dark-haired doctor who was just here, the one who was working on my prisoner—"

"You mean Dr. Graywolf?" the older man asked.

Well, ain't that a kick in the head? Conroy and his people had blown up the exhibit because of contempt for the people it honored and here he was, his life in the hands of one of the very people to whom he felt superior.

Graywolf. She rolled the name over in her mind. It sounded as if it suited him, she thought. He looked like a wolf, a cunning animal that could never quite be tamed. But even a cunning animal met its match.

Lydia nodded. "That's the one. He just took my prisoner upstairs to be operated on—where was he going with him?"

"Fifth floor," the man told her. "Dr. Graywolf's a heart surgeon."

A heart surgeon. Before this is over, Dr. Graywolf might need one himself if he doesn't learn to get out of my way, Lydia vowed silently as she hurried back to the bank of elevators.

Chapter 2

Lydia looked around the long corridor. After more than three hours, she could probably draw it from memory, as she could the waiting room she had long since vacated.

Blowing out an impatient breath, she dragged her hand through her long, straight hair. It was at times like this that she wished she smoked. Or practiced some kind of transcendental exercises that could somehow help her find a soothing, inner calm. Pacing and drinking cold coffee to which the most charitable adjective that could be applied was godawful, didn't begin to do the trick.

She knew what was at the root of her restlessness. She was worried that somehow John Conroy would manage to get away, that his condition wasn't nearly as grave as that tall, surly doctor had made it out to be. And when no one was looking, he'd escape, the way Lockwood had. Jonas Lockwood had been the very first prisoner she'd been put in charge of. His escape had almost cost her her career before it had begun.

She and Elliot had managed to recapture the fugitive within eighteen hours, but not before Lockwood had seriously wounded another special agent. It was a lesson in laxness she never forgot. It had made her extra cautious.

Something, she had been told time and again by her mother, that her beloved father hadn't been. Had Bryan Wakefield been more cautious with his own life, he might not have lost it in the line of duty. The ensuing funeral, with full honors, had done little to fill the huge gap her father's death had left in both her life and her mother's.

Lydia crumpled the empty, soggy coffee container in her hand and tossed it into the wastebasket.

The corridor was almost silent, and memories tiptoed in, sneaking up on her. Pushing their way into her mind.

She could still remember the look on her mother's face when she'd told her that she wasn't going to become a lawyer because her heart just wasn't in it.

Lydia smiled without realizing it. Her heart had been bent on following three generations of Wakefields into law enforcement. Her great-grandfather and grandfather had both patrolled the streets of Los Angeles and her father had risen to the rank of detective on the same force, doing *his* father proud.

Her mother had argued that she could become part of the D.A.'s office. That way, she would still be in law enforcement, only in the safer end of it. But Lydia had remained firm. Sitting behind a desk with dusty books or standing up in court in front of a judge whose bout of indigestion or argument with a spouse might color the rulings of the day was not for her.

With tears in her eyes, her mother had called her her father's daughter and reluctantly given her blessing while praying to every saint who would listen to keep her daughter safe. Lydia had no doubt that her mother bombarded heaven on a daily basis.

Mercifully, Louise Wakefield remarried six months after Lydia had successfully completed her courses at Quantico. Her stepfather, Arthur Evans, was a kind, genteel man who ran a quaint antique shop. Her mother made him lunch every day and always knew where to find him and what time he'd be home. It was a good marriage. For the first time in nearly thirty years, Lydia knew her mother was at peace.

Lydia looked at the wall clock as she passed it. She sincerely wished she could lay claim to some of that peace herself right now. Glancing at the clock again, she frowned. It announced a time that was five minutes ahead of her own watch. Not that it mattered in the larger scheme of things. It just meant that her prisoner had now been in surgery for three hours and forty minutes, give or take five.

She rotated her neck and felt a hot twinge in her shoulder. It had been bothering her the entire time she'd been here. She couldn't wait for this night to be over. All she wanted to do was to go and soak in a hot tub.

It was her bullet they were digging out of Conroy. If he hadn't moved the way he had, it would have been lodged in his shoulder, not his chest. Though she was filled with loathing for what he'd done, she'd only meant to disarm him. Cornered, the man had trained his weapon on Elliot. There'd been no time to debate a course of action. It was either shoot or see Elliot go down.

Lydia felt no remorse for what had happened. This kind of thing went with the territory and she had long ago hardened her heart to it. If there was pity to be felt, it went to the parents of the boy whose life had been lost and to the people who, simply going about their business, had been injured in the blast.

Lydia sighed. The world seemed to be making less sense every day.

She found herself in front of the coffee machine again. If she had another cup, she seriously ran the danger of sloshing as she moved. But what else was there to do? There was no reading material around and even if there had been, she wouldn't be able to keep her mind on it. She was too agitated to concentrate.

Digging into her pocket, she winced. Damn the shoulder anyway. It felt as if it was on fire. Probably a hell of a bruise there. When she'd shot him, Conroy's weapon had discharged as he'd fallen to the ground. She'd immediately ducked to keep from getting struck by the stray bullet. As near as she could figure, she must have injured her shoulder when she hit the floor.

Lydia glanced down at herself. The jacket and pants she had on were both discolored with the prisoner's blood. Shot, he'd still tried to put up a fight. It had taken Elliot and her to subdue him. For a relatively small man, Conroy was amazingly strong. She supposed hate did that to you.

She looked accusingly at the operating room doors. Damn it, what was taking so long? Were they rebuilding Conroy from the ground up?

Lydia stifled a curse. She knew she could have someone from the Bureau stationed here in her place, but she didn't want to leave until she had a status report on the bomber's condition. She wanted to know exactly what she was up against. There was no way she was going to lose this one, even for a blink of an eye.

Her stomach rumbled, reminding her that not even she could live on coffee alone. She tried to recall when her last meal had been. The day had taken on an endless quality.

Lydia jerked her head around as she heard the operating room doors being pushed open. The sound of her heels echoed down the corridor as she quickly returned to her point of origin.

The physician who had given her such a hard time emerged, untying his mask. He looked tired. That made two of them.

"Well?" she demanded with no preamble.

It didn't surprise Lukas to find the blonde standing here like some kind of sentry. Gorgeous, the woman still bore a strong resemblance to a bull terrier, at least in her attitude. Their earlier exchange had convinced him that she wasn't someone who would let go easily. Or probably at all, for that matter.

Lukas took his time in answering her, walking over to the row of seats in the waiting area and sinking down onto the closest one. The woman, he noted, remained standing.

"Well, is he alive?" she pressed.

Lukas pulled off his surgical cap and looked at her. "Yes. He's lucky. The bullet was very close to his heart. Less than a sixteenth of an inch closer and he'd be on a slab in the morgue."

Her mouth twisted. Whether the word lucky was appropriate or not was a matter of opinion. "Too bad the boy his bomb blew up wasn't as lucky."

Lukas didn't feel like being drawn into a debate. Weary, he rose to tower over the woman. It gave him an advantage. He found he preferred it that way. "Look, I don't want to know what he did. My job is to patch him up as best I can."

Her eyes grew into small points of green fire. "How can you not care?" she asked heatedly. "How can you just divorce yourself from the fact that the

man you just saved killed a teenage boy? That he
might have killed more people had his timing been a
little more fine-tuned.''

The woman was a firebrand. The kind his uncle
always gravitated toward. Too bad Uncle Henry
wasn't here to appreciate this, Lukas thought.

''Because I'm a doctor, not a judge and jury.'' The
look in his eyes challenged her. He knew all about
hasty judgments. ''Are you sure you have the right
man?''

She laughed shortly. The tip they had gotten had
specifically named John Conroy as the mastermind
of the new supremacy group whose goal was to
''purify'' the country. The explosives they'd found in
his house erased any doubts that might have existed.
What they hadn't found, until it was too late, was the
man himself.

''Oh, I'm sure.''

There was something in her voice that caught his
attention. ''That was your bullet I took out.''

''Yes.'' And he was going to condemn her for it,
she thought. She could see it coming. There was a
time for compassion and a time for justice. This was
the latter. Lydia raised her chin. ''We chased him
down into the rear loading dock behind the mall. I
shot him because he was about to shoot my partner.''

The hour was late and he should be on his way.
But something kept Lukas where he was a moment
longer. ''I didn't ask you why you shot him. Figured
that was part of your job.''

She didn't like the way he said that. "You weren't there."

"No, I wasn't. Now if you'll excuse me, I have a life to get back to. Or at least a bed."

Finished, he brushed past her and accidentally came into contact with her shoulder. The woman bit back a moan, but he heard it. Lukas stopped and took a closer look at the bloodied area around her shoulder. When she'd first come in, he'd assumed that the blood belonged to the prisoner. Now he had his doubts.

"Take your jacket off."

Startled by the blunt order, she stared at him. "What?"

"I thought that was pretty clear." There was a no-nonsense tone to his voice. "Take your jacket off," he repeated.

Even as a child, she had never liked being ordered to do anything. It raised the hairs on the back of her neck. "Why?"

The last thing he wanted right now was to go head-to-head with a stubborn woman. "Because I think that's your blood, not his."

Lydia turned her head toward her shoulder. Very gingerly, she felt the area around the stain. Flickers of fire raced up and down her arm. Now that he said it, she had a sinking feeling he was right.

Dropping her hand, she gave a dismissive shrug with her uninjured shoulder. "Maybe you're right. I can take care of it."

Lukas glanced over her head. The operating room

was free now. The orderly had wheeled his patient into the recovery room. Administration had sent in a security guard to watch him. That should please Ms. Law and Order, he thought.

"So can I. Come with me." It wasn't a suggestion. He caught her hand and dragged her behind him.

She had no choice but to accompany him. "You have a real attitude problem, you know that?"

Lukas spared her a glance. "I was going to say the same thing about you." He released her hand and gestured toward a gurney. "Sit there."

Lydia looked around the empty room, panic materializing. "Where's the prisoner?"

Opening a drawer in a side cabinet, he took out what he needed. "They took him to recovery."

Lydia turned on her heel, about to leave by the rear door, the way she assumed Conroy had. "Then I have to—"

He caught her hand again. This woman took work, he thought.

"Stay right here and let me have a look at that shoulder before it becomes infected," he instructed. "Relax, your prisoner's not about to regain consciousness for at least an hour."

She frowned, torn. Her shoulder was beginning to feel a great deal worse now than it had earlier. "You know that for a fact?"

The surgical pack in place, Lukas slipped on a pair of latex gloves. "Pretty much."

Maybe she was overreacting, at that. "Is he still handcuffed to the railing?"

In reply, Lukas nodded toward the metal bracelets lying on the countertop. "They're right there." He saw her look and watched her face cloud over. Like a storm capturing the prairie. "I figured you might be needing these for someone else."

She bit back a curse. Unconscious or not, she would have felt a great deal better if Conroy were still tethered to the railing on his bed. "This isn't a game."

"No one said it was." He nodded at her apparel. "Now take your jacket off. I'm not going to tell you again."

Tell, not ask. The man had a hell of a nerve. Setting her jaw, Lydia began to shrug out of the jacket, then abruptly stopped. The pain that flared through her left shoulder prevented any smooth motion. Acutely aware that the physician was watching her every move, she pulled her right arm out first, then slid the sleeve off the other arm. She tossed the jacket aside, then looked at her blouse. It was beyond saving.

She sighed. The Wedgwood blue blouse had been her favorite. "What a mess."

"Bullets will do that." Very carefully, he swabbed the area and then began to probe it. He saw her eyes water, but heard no sound. The woman was a great deal tougher than he'd assumed. He knew more than a couple who would have caused a greater fuss over a hangnail. "How is it you didn't realize you were shot?"

She measured out every word, afraid she was going to scream. "The excitement of the moment," she guessed. "I hit the floor when he fired. I just thought I banged my shoulder." Lydia sucked in a breath, telling herself it would be over soon. "It wouldn't have been the first time."

"And not the first time you were shot, either," he noted as he began to clean off the area. There was a scar just below her wound that looked to be about a year or so old.

Lydia pressed her lips together as she watched him prepare a needle. "No, not the first. What's that for?"

"That's to numb the area. I have to stitch you up." He injected the serum. "How many times have you been shot?"

She hated needles. It was a childhood aversion she'd never managed to get over. Lydia counted to ten before answering, afraid her voice would quiver if she said something immediately.

"Not enough to make me resign, if that's what you mean."

He couldn't decide if she was doing a Clint Eastwood impression or a John Wayne. Tossing out the syringe, Lukas reached for a needle. "You have family?"

Watching him sew made her stomach lurch. She concentrated on his cheekbones instead. They gave him a regal appearance, she grudgingly conceded.

"There's my mother and a stepfather." She paused to take a breath. "And my grandfather."

That made her an only child, he thought, making another stitch. "What do they have to say about people playing target practice with your body?"

Did he think she was a pin cushion? Just how many stitches was this going to take? "My mother doesn't know." She'd never told her mother about the times she'd gotten shot. "She thinks I live a charmed life. My father was killed in the line of duty. I don't see any reason to make her worry any more than she already does."

Lukas glanced at her. She looked a little pale. Maybe she was human, after all. "What about your grandfather?"

"He worries about me." Lydia kept her eyes forward, wishing him done with it. "But he's also proud. He walked a beat for thirty years."

"So that makes you what, third generation cop?"

"Fourth," she corrected. "My great-grandfather walked the same beat before him." Lydia looked at him sharply. He was asking an awful lot of questions. "Why? Does this have to go on some form, or are you just being curious?"

Lukas took another stitch before answering. "Just trying to distract you while I work on your shoulder, that's all."

She didn't want any pity from him. "You don't have to bother. It doesn't hurt."

He raised his eyes to her face. "I thought FBI agents weren't supposed to lie."

His eyes held hers for a minute. She relented. "It doesn't hurt much," she amended.

He knew it had to hurt a lot, but he allowed her the lie without contradiction. "That's because the wound was clean." He paused to dab on a little more antiseptic. It went deep. "The bullet cut a groove in your shoulder but didn't go into it. That's why you probably didn't realize it. That and, as you said, the excitement of what was happening. They say that when Reagan was shot, he didn't know it until someone told him."

It felt as if he was turning her arm into a quilting project. Just how long was this supposed to take? The last time she'd been stitched up, the doctor had hardly paused to knot the thread. "Maybe I should run for president then."

The crack made him smile. "Maybe. You'd probably get the under-twenty-five vote. They don't examine things too closely."

Another slam. Did he get his kicks that way? Or was it because she didn't crumble in front of his authority? "Anyone ever tell you your bedside manner leaves something to be desired?"

He found that her feistiness amused him despite the fact that he was bone-weary. "Most of my patients are unconscious when I work on them." He cut the thread. "There, done."

Gingerly, she tested her shoulder, moving it slowly

in a concentric circle. She felt the pain shoot up to her ear. "It feels worse."

"It will for a couple of days." Rising, he set the remaining sutures aside, then preceded her to the door. He held it open for her. "If you ride down to the first floor with me, I'll write you a prescription."

She paused long enough to pick up her now ruined jacket before following him to the door. "I told you, I don't need anything for the pain."

He began to lead the way to the elevators, only to find that she wasn't behind him. "But you might need something to fight an infection."

She looked down at her shoulder, then at him accusingly. "It's infected?"

"The medicine is to keep that from happening," he told her, coming dangerously close to using up his supply of patience.

"I have to go guard the prisoner." And to do that, she needed to know where the recovery room was located. She had a feeling he wasn't going to volunteer the information.

She was right. "There's a security guard posted outside the recovery room. You need to get home and get some rest."

The security guards she'd come across were usually little more than doormen. They didn't get paid enough to risk their lives. Conroy was part of a militant group, not some misguided man who had accidentally blown up a chem lab. "You ever watch 'Star Trek'?"

The question had come out of the blue. "Once or twice, why?"

"Security guards are always the first to die."

"Your point being?"

"Someone professional needs to be posted outside his room," she told him impatiently.

That was easily solved. "So call somebody professional." He saw her open her mouth. "As long as it's not you." The issue was non-negotiable. "Doctor's orders."

Certainly took a lot for granted, didn't he? "So now you're my doctor?"

Taking her good arm, he physically led her over to the elevator bank.

"I patched you up, that makes me your doctor for the time being. And I'm telling you that you need some rest." He jabbed the down button, still holding on to her. "You can bend steel in your bare hands tomorrow after you get a good night's sleep."

She pulled her arm out of his grasp, then took a step to the side in case he had any ideas of taking hold of her again. "Look, thanks for the needlepoint, but that doesn't give you the right to tell me what to do."

"Yeah, it does." The elevator bell rang a moment before the doors opened. He stepped inside, looking at her expectantly. She entered a beat later, though grudgingly, judging by the look on her face. "Your mother has gray hair, doesn't she?"

"Does yours?"

He inclined his head. "As a matter of fact, it's still midnight-black." After writing out a prescription for both an antibiotic and a painkiller, he tore the sheet off the pad.

"Then you must have left home early." She folded the prescription slip he had handed her. "I'll fill this in the morning."

"The pharmacy here stays open all night. I'll ride down with you if you like."

He certainly was going out of his way. But then, she knew what it was like to be dedicated to getting your job done. She couldn't fault him for that. "I thought you had a bed you wanted to get to."

"Like your prisoner, it's not going anywhere." He pressed the letter *B* on the elevator keypad. "A few more minutes won't matter."

Lydia had always been one to pick her battles, and she decided that maybe it would be easier just to go along with this dictator-in-a-lab coat than to argue with him.

With a sigh, she nodded her head in agreement as the elevator took them down to the basement.

Chapter 3

The scent of vanilla slowly enveloped her, began to soothe her.

Ever so slowly, Lydia eased herself into the suds-filled water. Leaning back, she frowned at her left shoulder. The cellophane crinkled, straining at the tape she'd used to keep the wrap in place.

Graywolf had warned her about getting her stitches wet just before she left him and, though she'd pretended to dismiss his words, she wasn't about to do anything that might impede her immediate and complete recovery. There was no question in her mind that she'd go stir crazy inside of a week if the Bureau forced her to go on some sort of disability leave. She had no actual hobbies to fill up her time, no books piling up on her desk, waiting to be read, just a few articles on state-of-the-art surveillance. Nothing she couldn't get through in a few hours.

Her work was her life and it took up all of her time. Yes, there was the occasional program she watched on television outside of the news and, once in a while, she took in a movie, usually with her mother or grandfather. There was even the theater every year or so. But for the most part, she ate and slept her job and she truly liked it that way. Liked the challenge of fitting the pieces of a puzzle together to create a whole, no matter how long it took.

It hadn't taken all that long this time, she thought, watching bubbles already begin to dissipate. The tip they'd gotten from Elliot's source had been right on the money.

Looking back, she thought, things seemed to have happened in lightning succession. An informer in the New World supremacy group they had been keeping tabs on had tipped off the Bureau that a bombing at a populated area was in the works. Initially, that had been it: a populated area. No specifics. That could have meant a museum, an amusement park, anyplace. For a week, with the clock ticking, they'd all sweated it out, having nothing to go on.

And then they'd gotten lucky. Very lucky, she thought, swishing the water lazily with her hand, letting the heat relax her. If that informant hadn't had a run-in with Conroy and been nursing a grudge against him, they would have never been able to piece things together. Even so, they'd gotten to the mall only seconds before the explosion had rocked the western end, the site that had just been newly renovated and expanded and had been filled with Native American art and artifacts.

As Elliot had driven through the city streets, trying to get there in time, she'd been on her phone, frantically calling the local police and alerting mall security to evacuate as many people as possible.

It been an exercise in futility. They'd reached the mall ahead of the police. She'd scanned the parking lot, taking in the amount of cars there, appalled at the number, even though by weekend standards, it was low.

The explosion had hit just as they'd parked. The force had sent one teenager flying into the air. He was dead by the time she'd reached him. It was then that she and Elliot had spotted Conroy running around the rear of what was left of that part of the structure.

She barely remembered yelling out a warning. All she could focus on was Conroy turning and aiming his gun in Elliot's direction. The rest had happened in blurry slow motion.

And try as she might, she still didn't remember being hit.

There were others involved; she knew that they were going to be caught. It was a silent promise she made to the teenager who wouldn't be going home tonight. Or ever.

Lydia sank down farther into her tub, the one luxury she had allowed herself when she moved in, replacing the fourteen-inch high bathtub with one that could easily submerge a hippo if necessary. Some people took quick, hot showers to wash away the tension of the day; she took baths when she had the time. Long, steamy, soul-restoring baths.

The phone rang, intruding.

Glancing at the portable receiver she'd brought in with her, Lydia debated just letting her machine pick up the call. But the shrill ringing had destroyed the tranquillity that had begun seeping into her soul.

Besides, it might be about Conroy.

Stretching, she reached over the side of the tub for the receiver and pressed the talk button. "Wakefield."

"Don't you ever say hello anymore?" The voice on the other end had a soft twang to it.

She smiled, sinking back against the tub again, envisioning the soft, rosy face, the gentle, kind eyes that were too often set beneath worried brows. "Hi, Mom. What's up?"

"Nothing, darling. I was just lonely for the sound of your voice."

Lydia knew evasion when she heard it. For now she played along. "Well, here it is, in its full glory."

"You sound tired."

Her mother was slowly working up to whatever had prompted her to call, Lydia thought. That was the difference between them. She pounced, her mother waltzed. Slowly. "It's been a long day."

There was just the slightest bit of hesitation. "Anything you can tell me about?"

Her mother knew better than that. "Just lots of paperwork, that's all," Lydia told her. Idly, she moved her toe around, stirring the water. Bubbles began fading faster. The scent of vanilla clung.

She heard her mother laugh shortly. "You lie as badly as your father did."

Lydia glanced at her shoulder to make sure it was still above the waterline. Keeping it up wasn't easy even if she was leaning against the soap holder.

"You don't want to know details, Mom." It was supposed to be an unspoken agreement between them. Her mother didn't ask and she didn't have to lie. Her mother was slipping. "All you need to know is that I'm okay. I'm soaking in a tub right now."

"Alone?"

Half asleep she still would have been able to hear the hopeful note in her mother's voice. "Yes, unless you count Dean Martin on the radio."

Her mother made no effort to silence the sigh that escaped. "Sorry, I was just hoping…"

She knew what her mother was hoping. It was an old refrain. "Mom, don't take this the wrong way, but not tonight, all right?"

"Something happened, didn't it? I heard about the bombing."

Here it comes, Lydia thought. The real reason for the call.

"Was that you—"

"Doing the bombing?" Lydia cut in cheerfully. "No." She decided to toss her mother a bone. Even the Bureau wasn't entirely heartless. "Doing the picking up of pieces? Yes. We've got a suspect in custody—that's all I can tell you."

There was disappointment and frustration in her mother's voice. "I can get more from the evening news, Lydia."

When she was small, her mother had been her first confidante. They would talk all the time. But she wasn't small anymore. On an intellectual level, she knew her mother understood why she couldn't say anything. It was the heart that gave them both trouble.

For a second her thoughts sidelined to the surgeon who had pushed her out of the operating room. Who had insisted on stitching her up. She forced her mind back to the conversation.

"They're at liberty to talk, Mom, I'm not. They don't have a possible case to jeopardize."

She heard her mother sigh. Louise Wakefield Evans had been both the daughter and the wife of a policeman. She, better than anyone, knew about procedures that had to be followed.

Still, she said, "I hate being shut out this way, Lydia."

Lydia shifted in the tub, then quickly sat up. She'd nearly gotten the bandage wet.

"I'm not shutting you out, Mom. I'm shutting evidence in." The water was turning cool. "Mom, I'm turning pruney, I'd better go."

Her mother knew when to take her cue. "All right. Good night, Lydia. I love you."

"Love you, too, Mom."

Before her mother could change her mind, Lydia pressed the talk button, breaking the connection and ushering in silence. She dropped the receiver onto the mat.

Lydia felt bad that she couldn't share what had happened to her today with her mother, but she knew it would only have served to agitate and worry Louise. In the long run, she'd rather her mother had semipeace of mind by remaining in the dark than live with daily terrors—even if she could give her details, which she couldn't.

Her mouth curved slightly as a question her mother had asked echoed in her brain.

Was she alone?

That would place her mother among the eternal optimists. Louise still nursed the hope that Lydia would be swept off her feet, marry and chuck this whole FBI special agent business.

Lucky for her, Louise hadn't seen that surgeon tonight. There was no doubt in Lydia's mind that her mother would have been all over Graywolf, plying him with questions, inviting him over for Sunday dinner. Louise Wakefield Evans was desperate for grandchildren and Lydia was the only one who could provide her with them. She'd had a brother, born first, but he had died before his first birthday, a victim of infant crib death syndrome. With no other siblings available, Lydia was the only one left to fulfill her mother's hopes.

"Sorry, Mom," Lydia murmured as she leaned forward to open up the faucet again.

The next moment, hot water flowed into the tub again, merging with the cooling liquid that was already there.

First chance she had, she was going to talk to Arthur about getting her mother a puppy. She knew her stepfather was sympathetic to her. A new puppy should occupy her mother, at least temporarily.

Closing her eyes, Lydia let her head fall back against the inflated pillow lodged against the back of the tub. An image of the surgeon materialized behind her lids.

Startled, she pried her eyes open.

What was she doing, thinking about him? She was supposed to be trying to make her mind a blank.

Maybe it was the medicine, making her woozy.

Lydia blew out a breath, ruffling her bangs. She decided that soaking in the tub might not be the smartest thing to do if she were truly sleepy. Death by Suds was not the way she wanted to go.

Lydia reached for a towel.

The rhythmic staccato of high heels meeting the freshly washed hospital floor had Lukas looking up from the chart he was writing on. Half a beat before he did, he knew it was her. He'd picked up on the cadence last night. Fast, no nonsense, no hesitancy. A woman with a mission.

Closing the chart, he replaced it on the nurse's desk, still watching the woman approach. He wondered vaguely if Ms. Special Agent was focused like that all the time or if it was the job that brought it out. Did she know how to kick back after hours? Did she even *have* "after hours"?

Lukas had a sneaking suspicion she didn't.

That made two of them.

Even after he'd gone home last night to catch a few hours of well-deserved sleep, he'd wound up calling the hospital to check on Jacob Lindstrom, the patient he'd operated on before Ms. Special Agent had thundered into his life.

Lukas's eyes swept over her as she walked toward him. The woman was wearing another suit, a powder blue one; but this time she had on a skirt instead of pants. The skirt brushed against her thighs as she walked and gave him the opportunity to note that her legs were as near perfect as any he'd ever seen. Long, sleek, and just curved enough to trigger a man's fantasies.

It made him wonder why Harrison hadn't hit on her last night. Special agent or not, she looked to be right up his best friend's alley.

But then, maybe Harrison *had* hit on her and she'd set him straight. That would have been a first. Lukas made a mental note to catch up with Harrison to ask for details when he got the chance. If there had been a conquest last night, something told him he would have known it. One way or another.

"You're here bright and early," he commented as she came up to him.

He didn't look as tired, she observed. His sharp, blue eyes seemed to be taking in everything about her. She'd always thought that Native Americans had brown eyes. "So are you."

Her mouth looked pouty when she said the word "you." Something stirred within him, but he dismissed it. He'd been around Harrison too long. Maybe the other man's ways had rubbed off on him. "I have patients to see."

Lydia inclined her head, as if going him one better. "I have a prisoner to interrogate."

And here, Lukas thought, was where they came to loggerheads. It hadn't taken long. Less than a minute, by his estimate.

"Not until he's up to it."

"If he's conscious, he's up to it, Dr...." Lydia paused and, though she knew his name, made a show of looking at the badge that hung from a dark blue cord around his neck. Since the back of the badge faced her, she turned it around. "Graywolf." Releasing the badge, she raised her eyes to his face. "This wasn't some spur-of-the moment, impulsive act by a deranged man acting out some sick fantasy. This was a carefully planned act of terrorism. This man is part of a group that call themselves the New World Supremacists. I assure you, he wasn't alone at the mall last night. I want to make sure his friends don't go scurrying off to their garages to concoct some more pipe bombs to kill more innocent people. The only way I'm going to do that is to get names."

He understood all that, but he was coming at this from another angle. He had to put the welfare of his patient first. "Ms. Wakefield—"

"That's Special Agent Wakefield," she corrected him. Taking out her wallet, she opened it for him. "It says so right here on my ID."

Holding her wallet for a moment, Lukas looked at the photograph. She looked better in person. The photograph made her look too hard, too unforgiving. There was something in her eyes that told him that might not be the entire picture.

He dropped his hand to his side. "I always wondered about that. Is 'special' a title, like lieutenant colonel?" he deadpanned. "Are there any regular, nonspecial agents at the agency?"

"We're all special," she informed him, finding that she was gritting her teeth.

"In our own way," he allowed magnanimously. "Even people accused of crimes."

Not in her book. "Just why are you yanking my chain, Doctor?"

Because it was there, he realized. But he gave her a more reasonable answer.

"Maybe it's because you insist on getting in my way. The man you shot almost died on the table last night. Twice. I'd like to make sure he doesn't. Having you go at him like a representative of the Spanish Inquisition isn't going to help his recovery. I think it might be better if you hold off asking any questions.''

Not hardly. And she didn't particularly like being told what to do. ''I don't give a damn about his recovery, Doctor. I just want him to live long enough to give me the names of his buddies.'' She watched him shiver and then turn up the collar of his lab coat. It wasn't particularly cold. ''What are you doing?''

''Trying to protect myself from frostbite.'' He slid his collar back into place. ''You always come off this cold-blooded?''

She could almost literally feel her patience breaking in two.

''I happen to be a very warm person,'' Lydia snapped, then realized how ridiculous that sounded coming in the form of a growl. A smile slowly emerged to replace her frown. ''Ask anyone.''

It was amazing. He wouldn't have thought that a simple smile could transform someone's face so much. But it did. The woman in front of him seemed light-years removed from the one he'd just been talking to. This one looked younger, softer. Way softer.

''Maybe I will.''

He was being nice. So why did she feel so uneasy all of a sudden? And why was he still looking at her as if he was dissecting her a layer at a time? ''What are you staring at?''

''Your smile.''

Instinctively she began to press her lips together to

blot out her smile, then stopped. The smile was replaced by a glare. "What's wrong with my smile?"

He spread his hands. "Nothing. Absolutely nothing. Makes you look like a completely different person, in my opinion."

As if she gave a damn about his opinion. "I'll remember that the next time I need a disguise." It was getting late and she had to get down to business. "Have you moved my prisoner since last night?"

She had remained long enough for Conroy to be transferred from recovery to a single-unit room, where she'd made certain that a policeman from the Bedford police force was stationed.

Lukas was about to remind her that the man was his patient before he was her prisoner, but he let the matter drop. He'd learned early on that butting his head against a stone wall never brought victory.

"I wouldn't dare. I left him just where I found him this morning."

She could do without the sarcasm. "How is he?"

It was Conroy's chart he'd been writing on when he heard her approach. "Still weak."

That was a relative term in her opinion. "I don't want him to dance, I just want him to talk."

"That might be difficult. He's on a great deal of pain medication—speaking of which," he segued smoothly, "how's your shoulder?"

Graywolf's question only reminded her of how much the shoulder ached. "If I was a bird, I'd have to postpone flying south for the winter, but under the circumstances, I guess it's all right.''

Lukas nodded. ''I need to see you back in a week to take the stitches out.'' She was favoring her left side. Would it have killed her to follow his instructions? ''I see you're not wearing a sling.''

She'd actually toyed with the idea this morning, arranging and adjusting several colorful scars around her arm and shoulder. They'd only made her feel like an invalid. ''I don't want to attract attention.''

Too late, Lukas thought. Three orderlies had passed by since she'd stopped to talk to him and all three had been in danger of severely spraining their necks as they turned to look at her. ''Then maybe you should wear a paper bag over your head.''

''What?''

Was she fishing for a compliment, or was she wound up so tightly about her job that she didn't see her own reflection in the morning? ''I'm just saying that a woman who looks like you do always attracts attention.''

Her eyes narrowed in surprise. ''Are you coming on to me, Doctor?'' She'd dabbled in profiling. Graywolf didn't seem the type.

''Me?'' He raised both hands, fingers pointed to the ceiling. ''I wouldn't have the nerve to come on to someone like you. I'm just making an observation, that's all.'' He looked at his watch. ''Now, if you'll excuse me, I've got the rest of my rounds to make.''

He was turning away from her when she called

after him. "You mean you're not going to hover over me while I try to question the prisoner?"

Lukas stopped to look at her one last time. "Would it do any good?"

A smile crept back to her lips as Lydia shook her head. "No."

"Then I won't." He crossed back to her, fishing into his coat pocket. He took out a card and pressed it into her hand. "There's my number if you need me."

She glanced down at the card. Three numbers were neatly printed above one another. "Pager, cell phone and office number." Lydia raised her eyes from the card. "What about your home number?"

"Unlisted. On a need-to-know basis," he added just before he left.

Looking after him, Lydia thoughtfully folded the card between her thumb and forefinger and tucked it into her jacket pocket.

"Damn but I never thought I'd live to see the day."

Roused from her thoughts, Lydia spun around to face Elliot. "See what day?"

He was grinning. *Wait until Janice hears about this!* "The day you were flirting."

"Flirting?" Lydia echoed incredulously. "Are you out of your mind? I was not flirting."

"No?" Elliot crossed his arms at his chest, waiting to be convinced. "Then what do you call it?"

"Talking."

"I see."

There were times when her partner got on her nerves—royally. "Don't give me that smug smile."

He made no attempt to eliminate it. "I wasn't aware that it was smug."

"Well it is," she told him. Because one of the nurses had stopped what she was doing and was obviously eavesdropping, Lydia pulled her partner aside, out of earshot. "What is this, a conspiracy? My mother calls to find out if I'm alone in the bathtub and then you come along and tell me you think I'm flirting."

Elliot made a mental note to later ask her what had prompted her mother's question. For now, he shrugged innocently. "Can't help it. In spring a person's mind often turns to thoughts of love, remember?"

What did that have to do with anything? "It's autumn. Remember?"

Unruffled, Elliot laughed. "I'm late, it's been a busy year."

Okay, she'd been a good sport long enough. This had to stop. "Elliot, I'm packing a gun."

The look he gave her was completely unimpressed. "I'm shaking."

This was getting them nowhere. And the day stretched out in front of her, long and unaccommodating. "Let's go, we have a prisoner to interrogate."

"Lead the way." Her partner's expression had turned appropriately serious, but there was a twinkle in his eye she had trouble ignoring.

Chapter 4

John Conroy was not a particularly large man. The height of five foot eight listed on his driver's license was charitably stretching the truth. Bandaged, bruised and buffered by white sheets in a bed, he looked small and non-threatening.

Looking at him, it was almost hard for Lydia to believe that this was the man who had helped to carry out an attack whose ultimate goal was to kill as many people as possible. Which made her wonder why he had picked a weeknight. Was it that he couldn't wait, or that he had thought there was less of a chance of being caught?

There was something to be said for impatience, she thought as Elliot closed the door behind them.

"Evil comes in all sorts of packages, doesn't it?"

Elliot commented, noticing the way she was looking at the man in the hospital bed.

"The Bible says that Satan was the most beautiful of all the archangels," she murmured, moving closer to the prisoner.

She noted with satisfaction that along with the various devices hooking Conroy up to vigilant monitors, a tarnished steel bracelet encircled his wrist, chaining him to the railing, keeping him from escaping if he could somehow summon the strength. She'd made a point of putting it back on him last night. Nice to see that the doctor hadn't removed it again.

Conroy looked as though he was unconscious. Lydia studied his face intently, watching for a telltale flutter of his lashes that would give his game away. There was none.

"Not that," she added, "this puny, unimpressive piece of work could have ever been remotely placed in that category."

Not getting a reaction to her insult, Lydia bent until her face was level with Conroy's.

Elliot came closer. "What are you doing?"

"Getting in his face." She spared her partner a momentary glance before looking back to Conroy. "Seeing if he's really unconscious. Are you, Conroy?" she asked loudly. "Are you really out, or just playing possum? Not going to do you any good, you know. You have to come up for air sometime."

Elliot laughed to himself. "Well, those golden tones would certainly rouse me right up." Finding a place for himself in the single-care unit, Elliot took a pistachio nut from his jacket pocket and began to work at it with his nails.

Straightening, she saw Elliot shell the nut. For as long as she'd known him, he'd always carried a supply of pistachio nuts in his pocket. With the understanding of a loving wife, Janice replenished his supply every morning. "Isn't it kind of early for that?"

He shrugged. "Gives me something to do." Seeing the wastebasket, he tossed the shell into it and took out another nut. "I think he's out, Lyd."

She nodded, annoyed. Frustrated. "Looks like the good doctor was right." So much for questioning Conroy now. Though Elliot had seniority, the assistant director had made her lead on this case. "Why don't you go back to the office and see about running down some of those phone calls that have been coming in? Take Burkowitz with you," she said, naming one of the agents appointed to the special task force. "And while you're at it, find out if the bomb squad has found something useful." She knew there'd been evidence galore, but whether or not it led anywhere was another story. Most of the time they were left with a plethora of puzzle pieces and no unifying tray to place them in. "No sense in both of us hanging around until Mr. Wizard here wakes up."

She'd get no argument from him on that. Elliot was already crossing to the door. "That might be a while, Lyd. Sure you want to hang around, waiting?" He'd never met anyone who hated waiting more than Lydia. "We could have Rodriguez page us."

He nodded toward the door and the man they had posted at the desk out front. It was one of their own now, instead of a local policeman, something the Bedford chief hadn't been overly happy about. As always, there was professional jealousy and the matter of jurisdiction clouding things up. But at bottom, they all wanted the same thing. Not to have this kind of thing happen in Bedford ever again.

She looked back at Conroy. Unlike Elliot's endless supply of pistachios, the supremacist was going to be a difficult nut to crack. She wanted to be sure that she got first chance at him. "I'd feel better being here."

After four years he could pretty much read her like a book. "Lyd, the bombing wasn't your fault."

Logically, no. But emotionally it was another story. "Thanks, but it might have been prevented if I'd been a little faster, dug a little deeper. We ignored that first rumor."

"Because it *was* a rumor, one of over a dozen— the rest of which were bogus," he reminded her. "Hell, Lyd, we had our hands full." He also knew her well enough to know that he was wasting his breath. "The term's 'special agent' not 'super agent.'"

The comment succeeded in evoking a smile from her. "Who says?"

Elliot had his hand on the door, and he was shaking his head. "You're getting more stubborn every day."

She looked at him significantly. "I had a damn good teacher."

"Haven't got the faintest idea what you're talking about," he deadpanned as he left the room.

Lydia heard the door close as she turned back to look at the man in the bed. He hadn't moved a muscle since they'd walked in. The only sounds in the room were the ones made by the machines arranged in a metallic semicircle around his bedside.

He looked almost peaceful. It made her physically ill to be in the same room with him.

"What kind of a sick pervert blows up women and children?" she demanded of the unconscious man in a low, steely voice that seethed with anger.

Only the sound of the monitor answered her question.

Impatient, she blew out a sigh. "You've got to wake up sometime," she told him. "And when you do, I'm going to be right here to squeeze the names of those other men out of you. You're going down for this, my friend, and you're not going down alone."

She knew that would be little comfort to the parents of the teenager who'd senselessly died, but maybe it would keep others from following Conroy's example. Lydia already knew for a fact that this kind of thing had never happened in Bedford before and she wanted to make sure that it never would again. She wanted to do more than send a message to the New World supremacy group who'd been behind this, she wanted to smash it into unrecognizable bits.

With Elliot gone, there was no one to distract her. Unable to remain any longer in the room with a man she loathed with every fiber of her being, she turned on her heel and walked out. She paused long enough to talk to the agent who was sitting at the desk less than five feet from the door.

"I want to know the second he opens his eyes, Special Agent," she told him. "Not the minute, the second. Clear?"

The dark head bobbed up and down. This was his first assignment. "Absolutely, Special Agent Wakefield."

Had she ever been that eager? she wondered. When she'd first come to the Bureau, had she seemed this wet behind the ears?

Somehow, she doubted it. There were times when she thought she'd been born old. At other times she knew it was her father's death and the job that had done this to her.

Her voice softened. "Do you have my pager number, Ethan?"

He looked surprised to be addressed by his given name rather than by the neutral title the Bureau had bestowed on all of its operatives. He patted his pocket where he'd put the card she'd handed him before she'd entered the hospital room. "Right here."

"I'm going to the cafeteria to get some coffee," she told the man. "Remember, the *second*."

He nodded solemnly.

Satisfied, Lydia walked down the corridor to the elevators. The cafeteria was located in the basement. Breakfast was probably still being served. Not that she really wanted any. She normally didn't eat until around noon, a holdover from her college days when she'd stayed in bed until the last possible moment. Then there would only be enough time to get to class. Food took second place to sleep.

This had all the earmarks of a long day, she thought. But Conroy had to come to sooner or later. With any luck, it would be sooner. She had every confidence that he could be broken and made to give up the names of the others. The man was small-time, small-minded; he wasn't going to want to go down alone.

One militant group down, only a million or so more to root out. When she thought of it in those terms, it was a daunting task. But a journey always begins with the first step and Conroy was their first step.

"So, did he say anything?"

Startled by the question coming from behind her, Lydia was caught off guard. She turned around, her hand to her gun before she recognized the deep, resonant voice.

Graywolf.

She relaxed, dropping her hand from the hilt of her weapon. "Are you following me?"

"You're walking around in my hospital," he pointed out. "These are my stomping grounds, not yours. And given that you're hovering around my patient, I'd say the odds are pretty good that our paths are going to cross with a fair amount of regularity." He crossed his arms in front of him. "You didn't answer my question. Did he say anything?"

For a spilt second the image of Lukas wearing full headdress, stripped down to fringed leggings and war paint, flashed through her mind.

Where had that come from? If there was anyone who didn't deal in stereotypes, it would be her.

Annoyed, unsettled, she shoved her hands into her pockets and lifted her shoulders in a moderate shrug that instantly reminded her she should be favoring the left one.

"You were right," she admitted grudgingly. "He was still unconscious."

A hint of a smile played along his lips. That had to cost her, he mused. She didn't strike him as someone who liked to admit she was wrong. He supposed if he were being honest, he could more than identify with that.

Lukas nodded. "Big of you to admit it. And I'll be equally big and not say I told you so. So, heading back to the office?"

"No, the cafeteria," she corrected. Since no elevator had appeared to rescue her from this conversation, Lydia pressed the down button again, harder this time. "I figure you have to have better coffee down there than in the vending machines."

A logical conclusion, but in this case, not a valid one. "Liquid tar would taste better than the coffee in the vending machines. Although if you really want better coffee..." He debated for a minute, then inclined his head. "Follow me."

She looked at him, not taking a step. "To where?"

Pausing, amused despite himself, he studied her. "You always this suspicious?"

Lydia raised her chin. "It's kept me alive so far."

The woman was definitely defensive. He wasn't aware that he had said anything to trigger that response. "The doctors' lounge on the first floor," he replied in answer to her initial question. "We keep a pot of the real stuff down there." Lukas began leading the way. This time, she followed. "How do you think we keep going all those hours?"

She shrugged indifferently. "Never gave it any thought."

He slanted a look at her. She had almost a perfect profile, he decided. "What do you give thought to?"

He was challenging her, she thought. "Ways to keep terrorists from blowing up innocent people."

He took her words apart. "What if they blow up guilty people?"

She sidestepped a couple coming out of a small gift shop, nearly walking into the large arrangement of sunflowers the man was carrying. "What?"

"In their minds," he explained, then backtracked

when he saw she wasn't following his conversation. Or maybe it was disapproval he saw on her face. "Maybe they think they're getting back at people who they feel are guilty of something."

Was he a bleeding heart? It didn't go with the image he projected. "Doesn't matter what they think. They're not supposed to act as judge and jury." She stopped abruptly. Maybe he *was* some sort of bleeding heart. What a waste that would be. "You're not defending the actions of these people, are you?"

He looked at her mildly. She couldn't read the expression in his eyes. He brought her to a bank of service elevators and pressed for one. It arrived before he took his finger from the button.

"No."

She stepped in ahead of him. He reached around her and pressed the ground floor button. "Then what are you doing?" she asked impatiently. She had no time for word games if that was what Graywolf was playing.

"Just trying to see how your mind works," he answered mildly. "Getting a dialogue going on your home territory."

"Why?"

"Because we're riding in an elevator together and I'd rather listen to you talk than put up with the music the hospital insists on piping in."

She had no idea why that made her feel like smiling. "So I'm better than a Musak tape?"

"At the very least." The elevator doors opened and

he took the lead again. "This way." He reached for her instinctively as two orderlies guided a gurney past them, heading in the opposite direction. Lukas noticed that she pulled away. "So how's your shoulder?"

"Sore."

He was surprised at the admission. He'd half expected her to say that she'd forgotten all about it. Maybe she was human, after all. This time, the thought made him smile.

"It's going to be that way for several days. I'll need to see you again in about a week to take out the stitches."

Lydia wasn't pleased with the idea of having to take off her blouse around him again. She knew he was a doctor, but there was something far too intimate about the whole thing.

"Won't they just dissolve on their own?"

He turned down another corridor. "They're not those kinds of stitches."

Where were they going, to Oz? Maybe this was a mistake. "Why not?"

"These hold better. The other kind we use for internal sewing." Reaching the lounge, he opened the door for her, then stopped. "Does this insult you?"

Lydia gave him a dismissive look as she walked by him. "If you're trying to be politically correct, it's too late for that," she informed him. "And no, having a man hold open a door for me doesn't send me off into an emotional tailspin." She tended to think of it in terms of equality. "If I'd gotten to the door first, I would have held it open for you."

"Fair enough." He crossed to the small island that housed a coffee machine and all the ingredients necessary to make a decent cup of smoldering caffeine. "How do you take your coffee? No, don't tell me," he interrupted himself. "Black, right?"

She wasn't a purist. She didn't drink coffee for the taste, but for what it could accomplish. "Depends on how bad it is."

"It's good."

The man, she realized, was standing too close to her. She liked having space around her, keeping everyone at a decent distance. Whether it was her training coming to the fore, or her own preferences, she never bothered analyzing. The end desire was still the same.

She took a step back. "Then black."

"Black it is," he replied.

Skittish, he decided, noting the way Lydia stepped back from him. As a boy, he'd seen a horse like that, a mare that had been mistreated. Winning her trust had been a challenge. He wondered how Ms. Special Agent would take to being compared to a skittish mare. Not well, if he was any judge.

She watched him pour rich, black liquid into one mug, then another. She assumed that the one he took was his. Accepting the other, she looked down at it. "Whose is this?"

"Someone who's not on duty right now." He took

a long sip from his mug. "He won't mind. Don't worry, it's clean," he assured her, amused. "He rinses it out once every fourth Wednesday of the month. That was last night, so you lucked out."

With a shrug, she took a long sip herself. The hot liquid cut a path through her insides. But he was right, it was good.

"You always this flippant?"

"No, actually I'm not. Must be the company." He looked at her significantly before sitting at the table to the left of the coffee station.

After a beat, she joined him. The table seated two and there wasn't all that much room under the table once he put his long legs beneath it. "How long before Conroy regains consciousness?"

He didn't even need to give the answer any thought. "Hard to tell."

She put her own interpretation on the answer. "Are you deliberately keeping him drugged?"

He set his mug down on the table. "Now why would I do that?"

She took the bleeding-heart scenario one step further. "So I won't interrogate him and possibly upset your precious patient."

He was actually more attuned to her feelings that he was letting on. There was something about her that had him rallying to the other side just to watch her reaction. He supposed there was possibly a small boy within him yet.

"He's my patient but he's far from precious." He

took another long sip and waited until the liquid hit bottom. "Don't get me wrong, 'Special Agent,' there's no love lost here. I don't pretend to cast a blind eye to what Conroy's done, but I've got to stay above my emotions when I'm doing what I was trained to do. Impartiality is what keeps me sharp." He studied her face. "I imagine it's the same for you."

"Sometimes." The way he looked at her made strange things happen in her stomach. She'd faced down a shooter who'd gunned down another special agent with far less activity transpiring below her waist. "And sometimes, I can't help feeling the way I feel. Passion is what spurs me on."

"'Passion,'" he repeated. He raised a brow. "Are you a passionate person, Special Agent?"

It took her a second to drag her eyes away from his lips. "Why do I feel you're mocking me every time you say that?"

His eyes held hers. "Could be because you're not comfortable with the title."

She ignored the small shiver that zigzagged down her spine, telling herself it was cool within the lounge. "Oh, but I am. See, you're not always right."

He shrugged, the soul of innocence. "Never claimed to be."

She redirected the conversation toward a topic she felt more comfortable with. "How long before Conroy can be transferred?"

To his ear, there was more than a little disdain in her voice. "To where, a dungeon?"

She resented what she took to be his condescending tone. "To a maximum security holding area in the county jail."

He finished his coffee and set down the mug. "Depends on how fast he responds and stabilizes."

She wrapped her hands around her own mug, her eyes intent on his face. If he lied, she thought she could detect it. "In your humble, expert opinion—"

His mouth curved slightly as he looked at her. "Now who's mocking who? And after I let you drink our coffee, too."

She didn't know if he was being sarcastic, or merely teasing. Lydia reserved judgment. "Turnabout is fair play. Answer the question."

"In my humble opinion," he repeated, "I'd say probably a week. Could be sooner." He looked at his empty mug, debating another serving. He'd already had four cups since he'd first opened his eyes this morning. "Could be longer."

He was giving her the runaround. She decided to goad him a little to see where it went. "Are you always this unsure of yourself?"

"I am never unsure of myself," he corrected. "I just don't try to second-guess my patients." Lukas raised a brow as he looked directly at her. "Even patients with fire in their eyes."

Lydia squared her shoulders. The action was not

without its price. "What are you trying to second-guess about me?"

"Why someone who looks like you would choose to put her life on the line every day."

Her back went up. She'd had to fight to overcome the handicap of her looks all her life. No one took her seriously at first, thinking that she'd gotten where she had solely because of her appearance. The Hollywood-perpetrated image of an empty-headed blonde was something she found herself fighting time and again.

"Instead of what, becoming a model?"

The barely veiled anger took him by surprise. And then he smiled slightly, understanding. She'd encountered prejudice. It gave them something else in common.

"That might be one way to go," he allowed. "I was thinking more along the lines of being a teacher, maybe making impressionable young boys study harder to make points with their beautiful instructor.

She relented, but only a little. "Now you're beginning to sound like my mother. I already told you last night, my father was a policeman. So was my grandfather and my great-grandfather."

Lukas studied her for a moment before saying anything. "So you went into the family business."

She looked up at the door as a man in a lab coat walked in. "So to speak." Lydia set down her mug. She was wasting time with small talk. "Look, is there any way to bring him to consciousness?"

Yes, there were ways, but Lukas thought it best to take a conservative approach. "We prefer to let nature take its course."

As far as she was concerned, that was nothing more than a convenient excuse. "Nature didn't operate on him last night, or pump him full of drugs."

"Nature needed a little kick start," he told her mildly. "But if it makes you feel any better, in all likelihood Conroy should be waking up in another couple of hours, although I don't think he'll be up to answering any questions. His mind will most likely be too fuzzy."

He *had* been giving her the runaround. "Why didn't you say so to begin with?"

"And miss the scintillating conversation we've just had? Not likely."

Lydia pressed her lips together to keep from telling him what she thought of him. "You know, I'm not sure I like you, Doctor."

He looked at her knowingly. "But I'm making you think, aren't I?"

Her eyes narrowed. "Among other things."

The sound of his resonant laughter curled into her empty stomach. Reminding her that she hadn't had breakfast yet.

Lydia rose to her feet. It was time to go. "Thanks for the coffee." She tossed the words off as she walked out through the swinging door.

Trevor Patrick, an eye surgeon and the other doctor Lukas had initially recruited to take part in his annual medical trips to the reservation, took the opportunity to sit in the seat Lydia had just vacated.

"Harrison was right." Lukas raised a brow, waiting for Trevor to explain. "That is one fine specimen of womanhood, Lukas."

"That she is, Trevor, that she is. But don't let her catch you saying that."

"Why?"

"Long story." Lukas rose. "And I've got patients waiting at the office. See you around."

Trevor watched him leave, a thoughtful expression on his face.

Chapter 5

Elliot looked up, surprised to see Lydia pushing the door open and briskly striding into the field office.

"What are you doing here?" He half rose in his chair in anticipation, ready to roll. "Did the suspect finally wake up?"

With more than a touch of disgusted disappointment, Lydia shook her head. Elliot sat again, silently repeating the first question he'd put to her by the way he looked at her.

With a fresh wave of adrenaline coursing through her veins thanks to both the coffee from the doctors' lounge and in a minor way, she supposed, from the doctor himself, Lydia had given John Conroy exactly fifteen minutes to wake up. When he hadn't, she'd renewed her previous instructions to the special agent on duty to call her the second the unconscious man moved so much as an eyelash and then left the hospital.

"Suspect," she echoed Elliot's term with contempt. "I hate calling him that when we've got the guy dead to rights."

Elliot wasn't all that crazy about the label himself, though he did acknowledge the need for it. "Makes everything equal," Elliot told her as he made himself comfortable behind the computer. The back injury that had sent him under the surgeon's knife and then to rehab for six weeks was beginning to act up. He reached for a painkiller.

Lydia noticed but pretended not to. "Not hardly," she muttered. "No, Conroy's still out. But I need to do something more useful than grow roots in the vinyl floor covering." She nodded toward the open door and the offices that were laid out down the corridor. "How's the crime scene investigation coming?"

Wondering the same thing, Elliot had just gotten off the phone with the head of that department of the Bureau less than ten minutes ago.

"They're still bringing the pieces in. I hear they've got enough fragments tagged to keep a team of five busy from now until Christmas."

Lydia frowned. Seeing as how it was September, that didn't sound overly promising.

"Great," she muttered under her breath. "How about something new on the man himself? Anything?"

"Nothing new, just the usual." He indicated the file he'd just compiled from various pieces of information he'd lifted from the local police database. "John Conroy's a wizard with explosives. The service loved him, then things went a little sour when he decided to be a maverick. Peacetime is hell for militant types. Didn't obey the rules, barely avoided a dishonorable discharge."

It was an old, familiar tune, one she'd heard more than once during her time with the Bureau.

"From the looks of it, he couldn't really find a niche for himself in civilian life." Elliot held up what looked to be a résumé. "He held down a string of jobs as a guard, which he got on the strength of his service record.

"His domestic life is a shambles, probably because of his beliefs. Divorced twice, most recently a year ago. Here's a tidbit you might find interesting." He swung the folder around one hundred and eighty degrees so that she could see for herself. "Says that his only daughter ran off with some guy she hooked up with from New Mexico. She died of a drug overdose this spring. The guy was Native American and 'daddy' highly disapproved."

"Seeing as how the New World group believes that only White Anglo-Saxon Protestants deserve to live in this country, I can see why. I guess the Native American exhibit sent him off the deep end."

Elliot knew she was just talking out loud, not looking for his input. "More than likely. But if it hadn't been that, he and his group might have set off a bomb in Little Tokyo, Figueroa Street, or for that matter, Knotts Berry Farm. I hear they have Native American dancers performing ritual dances every day." He took the folder back. "You never know with types like that."

But it was their job to know, to crawl into the minds of terrorists, be they foreign or domestic, to discover what it was that started the whole dreadful process by which lives were lost and property destroyed. In the back of the mind of every special agent attached to the terrorist division was the specter of another World Trade Center or Oklahoma City bombing.

"Find out everything you can about Conroy. Who his friends in the service were, who he hangs around with. Somewhere in there has to be the names of the people responsible for this." She knew she was asking him to find needles in a haystack, but they needed those needles. "Put everything down, no matter how small." She smiled as she recalled something he had said to her on their very first investigation together. "No information is extraneous in the long run, remember?"

Elliot sighed. "I've got to learn to keep my mouth shut around you."

She laughed. He'd been her partner for four years, she'd been to his house for dinner countless time, played with his children, kept vigil and comforted his wife when he'd gone under the knife to correct a back problem. There was a bond between them that transcended their professional relationship. She knew him inside and out. As he did her.

"Never happen. You'd explode."

Elliot looked over the rim of the glasses he'd only recently been forced to wear for close-up work. "A little respect for your elders."

"Ten years does not make you my elder, Elliot," she scoffed, rising. "It just gives you more candles to blow out on your birthday cake, that's all."

He turned his chair to get a better view as she paused in the doorway. "And just what are you going to be doing while I'm doing all this mind-numbing research and legwork, Oh fearless leader?"

She jerked her thumb down the corridor just beyond the door. "Well, for one thing, I'm going to see what the diligent people at the bomb investigation unit have come up with for me. Maybe we'll get lucky and can trace where he bought the detonating devices. Better yet, maybe he didn't buy it and one of his group did. Oh, and one more thing." She paused in the doorway. "See if you can get a line on your snitch."

"So far, I haven't been able to contact him."

"Keep trying."

He nodded. There was no question that Lydia worked harder than any three people he knew, but that didn't stop him from pretending to complain about his own workload. "Next time Zane asks for lead, remind me to raise my hand first."

"Next time," she echoed with a nod of her head as she walked out.

As someone who had suddenly become aware that they had fallen asleep without meaning to, Lydia realized that her mind wasn't on her work. Somehow, while she had been trying to understand the lengthy technical data reports spread out in front of her, her thoughts had strayed to the tall, imposing surgeon who had been able to pull Conroy through.

It wasn't like her to not focus on her work, but then, maybe she'd been too focused and this was her mind's way of telling her she desperately needed a break. The data had begun to swim before her eyes.

Exhausted, Lydia rose from behind the cramped computer desk where she was sitting and stretched. She needed air and food, and she wanted to feel a little like a human being again rather than some kind of a machine that processed information, searching for the piece that would pull everything together.

What she needed most of all, she thought grudgingly, was a break in this case. She was always dogged about her assignments, but this one was going to haunt her for a long time. The boy was already dead when she'd reached him, but his eyes seemed to have looked straight at her. It may be cliché, but she felt as if his spirit wouldn't rest until she brought all the people involved in the bombing to trial.

To make things worse, Elliot still hadn't been able to reach the man who had provided them with their lead in the first place. She had a very bad feeling about that.

Just as she rose to her feet, feeling an annoying stiffness in the shoulder that had been wounded, her pager came to life. Glancing at it, she recognized the number on the screen. Rodriguez.

"You going somewhere?" Elliot asked as he walked in with two huge, covered, containers of coffee he'd just bought at the new café on the next corner. The chain of coffee shops, he'd commented to her earlier, seemed to be multiplying like rabbits, with stores springing up all over.

"Rodriguez just paged us." Grabbing the jacket she'd long since discarded, she pulled it on while simultaneously digging out her cell phone. She didn't want to waste any time calling Rodriguez from the office when she could do it on her way to the hospital. "The 'suspect' is either awake, or dead. In either case, it's a change."

Elliot set the containers down on his desk. "Want me to come with you?"

Elliot was beat, she could see that. He still hadn't fully recovered from the surgery that had landed him on a six-week medical disability leave, and the hour was late. "I can handle it. You close up for the night here." She was already at the door. "I'll call you later if there's anything to report."

Elliot had been with the Bureau for more than fifteen years. He didn't like being maneuvered into the background, even when he knew the motive behind it. "You don't have to baby me, Lyd."

In a hurry, she paused in the doorway to look at her partner. She hadn't meant to wound his pride. "I know, that's Janice's job." There was affection in her voice. "Go home and let her do it."

"And who's going to baby you when the time comes?"

Lydia was grateful that he didn't know about the wound Graywolf had sewn up for her. There was no question in her mind that if he did, Elliot would pull seniority and go in her place.

"The person hasn't been born who's man enough for the job," she called over her shoulder before she finally hurried out.

Elliot could always make her smile, she thought. And he was right, she was babying him. She would have balked if anyone had tried it with her. But there were extenuating reasons for that. She was determined to stand up for herself. This was still, by and large, a man's world and she had to work twice as hard to get one half the respect a man would get. That meant being on top of things and finding the answers first.

And never letting her guard down, the way her father had for that split second that had cost him his life, she thought darkly as she hurried into the parking structure for her vehicle.

He'd died on a day like this, dark and rainy. Died

on a day like this and was buried on a day like this. Rain always made her feel sad and lonely.

She tried to shrug off the feeling as she got behind the wheel of her '99 silver Honda.

The mild drizzle was a full-fledged storm by the time she'd driven her car out onto Santa Ana's city streets. Logically, she knew that after several dry years, they could certainly stand the rain, but that didn't mean she had to like it. Besides, for the most part, native Californians always acted as if rain was some kind of plague sent down to chastise them for transgressions, and they drove as if they were trying to escape the drops as quickly as possible. Accidents always doubled on rainy days.

Tension infused her body as she drove to the hospital. She decided to postpone calling Rodriguez until she was almost there. No sense in taking unnecessary chances.

Despite the unexpected storm, Lukas found the day to be uneventful and tranquil. There'd been no life-saving surgeries to perform, no patients to rescue from the jaws of death. The most exciting thing he'd encountered in his day, he had to admit, had been the special agent with the attitude. Thinking of her made him smile.

As he filled out his reports, he thought of another determined, dedicated woman—his mother. He decided to take time during his lunch period to call her.

A far more dutiful son now that he had entered his

third decade of life than he had been during the other
two, especially his early teen years, Lukas had begun
to understand his mother more and more and to appreciate the sacrifices she'd made to give him the kind
of life he'd aspired to and ultimately achieved.

"What's wrong?" she asked the moment she'd recognized his voice on the phone. "Are you sick?"

If he closed his eyes, he could see her sitting in the
tiny office that served as a teachers' lounge and prin-
cipal's office all in one. Her thick black hair, still
without any flecks of gray and plaited in two long
strands, reached almost to her waist. Very much the
modern woman, she was most comfortable in her native dress and always taught school that way.

"Don't worry so much, Mother. If I was, I could
heal myself. I'm a doctor, remember?"

"Remember?" Juanita Graywolf laughed softly.
"How could I forget? It took my holding down two
jobs for twelve years to get you there."

He fully appreciated that and wished she would let
him take care of her now. Or at least have her agree
to slow down. Her concession to his entreaties had
been to relinquish her second job and retain only one.
The one she adored. Teaching at the reservation
school.

Before he could say anything else to her, she repeated, "Why are you calling?"

"Do I need a reason?"

"Need one, no. Usually have one, yes." He heard
a bell ringing in the background. Lunch was over. The

children would be filing into her small classroom soon. "So, what's up?"

It was good to hear her voice. It occurred to him that he hadn't seen her in some time. How did life keep getting so busy? "Nothing, I just ran into someone who kind of reminded me of you, that's all. Stubborn, plows right through everything, knows best."

There was a smile in her voice. "Sounds like a lovely woman."

"I didn't say she was a woman." But he might have known she'd figure it out.

"You didn't have to. You said the person reminded you of me. If it had been a man, you wouldn't have thought to call."

"Maybe I would have," he countered, absently looking at his calendar. September. What happened to his summer? "I'm overdue."

"Yes, I know. And right now, so am I." He could hear voices behind her. Young voices. "Call me tonight. Or better yet, tomorrow night. Your uncle's going off on a fishing trip and I'll be alone. It'll be nice to hear another voice."

"You've got it, Mother," he promised. "Talk to you then."

"I'll hold you to that." There was a slight hesitation. "Lukas, nothing's wrong is it?"

"No, nothing." He could probably never cure her of worrying. But then, he'd given her a great deal to be worried about when he was younger: running with the gang on the reservation, collecting him at the local jail for joyriding in a vehicle that, unknown to him, one of the other boys had stolen. "Really."

"Good. I'll be waiting tomorrow night." With that, she hung up.

Lukas smiled to himself as he returned the receiver to its cradle and reached for his umpteenth cup of coffee. Pulling it closer, he settled back to dictate the notes he'd made while examining Mrs. Halloway. Eighty-seven years old and the heart of a young cheerleader. She made a semi-annual pilgrimage to his office at the insistence of her children and grand-children—and to flirt with him. He only hoped that he was half as energetic when he reached her age.

He paused when he realized that he'd dictated "Wakefield" instead of "Halloway" into the ma-chine. Lukas rewound the tape to the point where he'd made his mistake. He was accustomed to strong, pow-erful women who took charge as if it were their God-given right. Coming from a matriarchal society, Lu-kas had encountered women of Special Agent Wakefield's persuasion since he'd begun walking and talking. He'd learned how to integrate his own life with theirs without losing any of his own self-respect or his convictions, or surrendering any of his mas-culinity. Rather than waste time butting heads, he chose other ways to get things done his own way.

He had to admit, though, that he hadn't encoun-tered someone like Lydia since he'd left the reserva-tion for good. There hadn't been anyone quite like her in the large world he'd been moving through since he graduated from medical school and earned his position on Blair Memorial's staff.

Maybe that was why he found himself thinking about her, why she seemed to linger on his mind, popping up during the course of the day. It made him think that perhaps she was someone who might bear further exploring, if for no other reason than nostalgia.

"In the meantime," he murmured, aware of the time, "Mrs. Halloway's notes aren't going to dictate themselves." He pressed the record button and began to dictate again.

Finished with his visits at the office and his rounds at the hospital for day, Lukas was on his way out, walking through the hospital lobby when he saw her.

Lydia had just entered the building. The phrase "woman with a mission" popped into his head again. Even with distance between them, he could see that determination was written all over her face. She'd burst into the lobby through the electronic doors a scant half a second after they began to open.

Amused, he quickened his pace and caught up to her. "What's up?"

Lydia jerked around. She was so focused on the reason for her return to the hospital that she hadn't seen him approach. Annoyed with the oversight, she silently upbraided herself. She was supposed to be aware of her surroundings at all times, not oblivious to them. She was going to have to work on that.

"Conroy's conscious," she told him, heading for the bank of elevators.

When she'd finally placed the call to Rodriguez from her car, he'd told her that Conroy had opened his eyes, but that he wasn't really awake or responsive. She figured by the time she arrived, the supremacist would be. If not, there were ways to help him along. She'd always regarded herself as a kind, fair person. But kindness abruptly terminated when it came face-to-face with a cold-blooded killer.

This was a new development, Lukas thought. When he'd looked in on Conroy earlier in the afternoon, the man had still been unconscious.

"Maybe I'd better come along then." There was nothing pressing waiting for him tonight beyond a program on television he wanted to catch at ten.

Lydia broke stride for a second before resuming her pace. "Why? To check up on me?"

For a woman who wasn't overly tall, she covered a lot of ground quickly. He lengthen his stride. "No, on him. Why, should I be checking up on you?" His gaze swept over her. "You don't look as if you're carrying any rubber hoses or brass knuckles on you."

She stopped at the elevator and jabbed the up button. She looked at him, annoyed. "How can you joke?"

"Because humor is what keeps us sane, Special Agent." The elevator car arrived and he followed her in, letting her press the button for their floor. "Tell me, if I get to know you any better, do I get to call you just 'Special'?''

She blew out a breath. Among other things, she'd done a little background research on Graywolf this afternoon, saying it was just to help fill in the gaps. What she'd learned had roused grudging respect. He'd come up the hard way, living on a Navaho reservation, raised by his mother and a maternal uncle after his father had died in less than noble circumstances. She also knew that Lukas had run with a bad crowd as a young teen before he'd abruptly turned around.

Maybe he felt some sort of kinship with the man they had in custody, something along the lines of "There but for the grace of God go I." Whatever it was, she didn't have time to let it get in her way.

"No," she replied tersely, wishing someone else had gotten on the elevator with them, "you can't." Lydia shifted slightly. It was entirely too confining in here with him.

His eyes seemed to look deep into her being and she found herself struggling not to fidget. That he could actually create this feeling within her annoyed her no end.

"Is that because you're not special or because I'm not privileged?"

She weighed her words carefully, pausing before answering. "A little bit of both, maybe."

The elevator stopped on the second floor, but no

one got on. Another car must have arrived just before
them, she surmised. Pity.

"What's your name?" Lukas asked her suddenly.
"You flashed your ID by me so fast, I didn't get a
chance to read it."

Why was this damn car stopping on every floor?
she wondered as it opened for the third floor. Again,
no one got on. "Wakefield."

"No, I mean your first name."

Lydia turned to look at him, debating the merits of
telling him. She had no idea why allowing him this
harmless piece of information felt suddenly as if she
were opening a door to something. Still, she couldn't
exactly refuse to tell him. That would have been
childish. Besides, it was written on her ID. "Lydia."

"Lydia," he repeated. "Pretty."

Was he going to make some inane comment about
her matching her name next? She stared straight
ahead, willing the elevator to bypass the fourth floor
and go straight to the fifth. It didn't.

"Never gave it any thought."

"It is," he assured her quietly. She felt something
rippling along her skin and wondered how a draft
could have gotten into the elevator. Mercifully, the
doors opened on five and she all but barreled out.

He kept abreast. "So, what's the plan, Lydia?"

She spared him a cold look, this man who had been
playing hide-and-seek with her thoughts today.
"Plan? There is no 'plan.' I ask questions, you stand
in the background. End of story."

"I'm not much for standing in the background."

His voice was low, quiet, and she had the unshakable feeling he was putting her on some kind of notice. Probably accustomed to having everything his way. Well, not in an FBI investigation.

She halted in front of the Coronary Care Unit door. "All right, stand anywhere you want, just not in my way. He's your patient, but he's my prisoner and as far as I see it, that takes precedence."

He stopped her just before she pushed open the door to the CCU, placing his hand over hers. "It doesn't take anything if he dies."

She dropped her hand and turned to face him. "What do you think I'm going to do, torture him until he talks?"

She was standing so close, he could smell the soap she'd used that morning, catch the light shampoo fragrance that clung to her hair. And feel the heat of her anger. A woman like this would be magnificent, he caught himself thinking. Under the right circumstances.

"I'm not sure what you're capable of, Special Agent Wakefield. But I think I'd like to find out."

Definitely on notice, she thought. She wanted to dress him down, but found that her tongue had suddenly turned leaden and uncooperative, as had her lips. And as for the thoughts suddenly coursing through her head, they had no place here, certainly not in an ongoing investigation. A small thrill fluttered through her, stubbornly refusing to go.

Just as stubbornly, she refused to acknowledge it. Like the flu, it would leave eventually. "Then watch, if you like. But unless he goes into cardiac arrest, stay clear."

Lukas inclined his head. "Yes, ma'am."

He was mocking her, but she would have to put him in his place later. Right now, nothing was more important than getting Conroy to talk.

Rodriguez rose from the chair he'd been occupying near Conroy's bed the moment she walked in, the magazine he'd been reading falling to the floor. "No change."

Lydia frowned, looking at the sleeping figure. "I thought you said he woke up."

"Like I said, he opened his eyes," Rodriguez verified. "Then closed them again."

Moving around Lydia, Lukas crossed to the bed and took readings from the monitors on either side of Conroy. "Vital signs are getting stronger," he told her.

"Good," she bit off. She looked at the man in the bed, his face a pale, milky white, the color making him all but blend with his pillow. "Are you awake, Conroy?" There was no indication that he heard her despite her clear enunciation. "I know about her, Conroy. I know about Sally."

Lukas was about to tell her that just because the man's signs were good didn't mean he was conscious when he saw John Conroy open his eyes and look directly at Lydia.

There was hatred in them.

Chapter 6

Color suddenly materialized in the form of wide streaks that continued to grow along Conroy's cold, pale skin. His eyes were fathomless in their darkness as they scowled at her. Lydia felt as if was looking into the face of pure evil.

"Leave Sally out of this!"

Yes! Triumph telegraphed its way through her. She's found a way to get to him. This had to be the key, but to what door? Watching his expression, Lydia moved cautiously—for Lydia.

"How would she have felt, knowing you did this terrible thing? That you picked a place where young kids hang out, maybe even some of her friends." According to the information they had, Sally had attended a local school before running off. "How would she have felt, knowing that her father could kill scores of people, scores of kids without any compunction—''

''How would she have felt?'' Conroy interrupted, raising his head from the pillow. His voice, sharp, angry, sounded as if it had torturously crawled up the length of his throat. ''Damn you to hell! She wouldn't have *felt* anything. She can't *feel* because she's dead! My daughter's dead, do you understand?'' Incensed, he tried to prop himself up on his elbows. Tubes tangled along his arms, pulling at their source. ''And those kids…those kids—''

Abruptly, the tirade stopped. The streaks along his skin had turned a bright red. His eyes suddenly glazed over and he clutched at his chest. The sound coming from his lips was a gurgling, strangling noise.

''Move!'' Lukas ordered. Not waiting for her to comply, he elbowed a stunned Lydia out of his way.

Lydia stumbled backward, half in response to his command, half from the force of his push. Her eyes never left the suddenly rigid features of the man who had just cursed her. The bright blue lines running across one of the monitors had all leveled out after spiking. Conroy's chest wasn't moving.

Lukas pressed a button beside the bed. A loud, jarring noise began echoing through the room and down the hall, declaring a Code Blue. In less than thirty seconds, two nurses, an orderly and an intern came running into the room. One of the nurses was pushing a crash cart.

The glass-enclosed room, one of twelve within the CCU, was small, with most of its space already eaten up by the monitors. It was filling to capacity.

Lydia jockeyed for position, trying to stay out of the way, but still within view of what was going on. With the others converging around Conroy, orders and hands flying, it was hard for her to see.

She could feel Rodriguez shifting behind her. "It's getting too crowded in here. Step out into the hall," she told the agent.

Despite all the commotion surrounding the patient, Lukas could still make out her voice. He injected a small dose of medication into Conroy's IV to stimulate the man's heart.

"Maybe you should do the same," he told her, raising his voice without looking up.

Lydia didn't waste time responding to the barely veiled order, or arguing her position. She quietly and stubbornly simply remained where she was. Watching. And praying that her zeal hadn't pushed Conroy over the edge. She needed him. Once he gave he what she wanted, the system could have him. Despite what Lukas had said to her the other day, she had no desire to act as judge and jury. That would put her in the same category as Conroy, a space she didn't want to occupy.

"I've got a pulse," one of the nurses declared. Her words were shadowed by the blue line on the monitor that transformed into a continuous steady wave as it snaked its way across the screen.

The pulse grew stronger.

The patient was going to live. At least for now. Lukas stepped back to let the others around him take care of the details. Stripping off the gloves he'd hastily pulled on, he looked at Lydia still standing by the entrance. Though she hadn't said a word, he'd known she was there. She wasn't a woman who could be ordered around, even in the heat of a life-and-death moment.

Tossing the gloves into the wastebasket, Lukas made his way around the milling bodies to her side. He wasn't feeling very magnanimous at the moment.

"That's twice you almost killed him. Maybe you should ask to be replaced before there's a third."

Choice words came rushing to her lips, but Lydia forced herself to swallow them, struggling to see things from his point of view. It was better to have allies than enemies; you never knew when you might need someone's help.

It wasn't easy, but she curbed her tongue. It was even harder to sound contrite, especially when what she truly regretted was not getting any answers.

"You're right." She forced the words out of her mouth. "It was too soon, I shouldn't have pushed so hard."

Though he was surprised at her admission, Lukas wasn't through being angry. If he hadn't been here, Conroy could have died. "Damn straight you shouldn't have. I can't have him getting excited."

So much for getting more flies with honey. "And

I can't have him, or any of his friends, blowing up shopping malls, or churches, or *hospitals* just because they don't like the people in them," she said heatedly. "Or whatever else they get it into their heads to blow up 'for the good of the country.'" The last phrase was a quote from the note she and Elliot had found in Conroy's garage that had tipped them off to the suspect's target. Beneath it had been a tirade about the drain people of color put on the country, except that the term Conroy had used hadn't been nearly as polite.

Lukas crossed his arms in front of him and looked at her solemnly as he worked at controlling his own anger.

She had an inkling of how his forefathers must have appeared, decked out in chief's regalia, glaring down at the white settlers in their fragile wagons as they crossed into the merciless Arizona territory.

At any other time, the irony of it all would have struck her as amusing.

"Right now, I don't think Conroy's in any condition to blow up a milk carton, much less anything else."

"But his friends are," she pointed out. "And they're the ones who got away."

Part of what had gotten him on the right path and ultimately off the reservation was cultivating a positive attitude. He reverted to it now, though not with a great deal of conviction. "Maybe they'll stop here. Maybe blowing up the mall was the point."

He was being incredibly naive, she thought. "And maybe not." In fact, she was willing to bet on it. "I can't take that chance. The people who live around here can't take that chance," she emphasized. "Besides, those so-called supremacists have got to be punished for what they did." She thought that he, of all people, would understand that. Didn't his tribe have some rule along the lines of the old biblical eye for an eye? "They can't just be allowed to get away with it. The Bureau can't say, 'Boys'll be boys, but just don't do it again.' That'll just open the floodgates for every whacko in the country to 'even the score,' or to push their own violent agenda."

"How do you know it's a boy?" he asked her quietly.

What was he doing, nit-picking now? "Boys, men, what's the difference?" She realized she'd raised her voice again when one of the nurses, the one who had brought in the cart, glanced at her. Lydia pressed her lips together, annoyed that this man kept making her lose her temper.

"A lot," he answered. And something within him suddenly wanted to show her exactly how different. "But that's not what I meant." He saw her raise a questioning eyebrow. "What makes you think there are no women involved in this bombing?"

A ready retort faded as she first opened her mouth to answer, and then shut it again. Damn him, he had a point. That should have occurred to her, not him. Granted there was all that profiling data to fall back on, but that didn't mean anything was written in stone. Things were only one way until they changed and were another.

Conceding the round to him, Lydia raised her eyes to his. "Want to join our team?"

His somber expression melted a little around the edges and then he laughed at the suggestion.

"Maybe in an advisory capacity." He grew serious again. "And my first piece of advice is, don't kill the golden goose. You're not going to get any eggs if you do."

"Aesop's Fables?" she asked in surprise. She would have expected something different from him. "Isn't there any comparable Navaho legend to bring the same point home?"

As soon as the words were out, she bit her lower lip. That was stereotyping, something she ordinarily wasn't guilty of. But then, he was her first Native American anything and she had grown up watching old-fashioned Westerns with her father on television. It wasn't an excuse, but it was a reason.

His eyes narrowed. Was she checking up on him? "How did you know I was Navaho?"

She gave him the truth, knowing he wouldn't stand for anything less. "Conroy's not the only person I researched last night."

Her honesty surprised him. The annoyance abated. "Afraid I'll blow something up?"

He didn't like having his privacy invaded, she thought. The funny thing was, she could wholeheartedly sympathize with that. But niceties had to take a back seat when terrorists and dangerous, bomb-wielding supremacists were concerned.

"No. I just like knowing who I'm dealing with. Fewer surprises that way."

He inclined his head, accepting the explanation. "You could try asking."

She didn't know him, yet she knew better. "Would you have told me?"

The smile that look his lips was slow. And unnervingly sensual as she watched it spread. "Maybe over dinner. Now we'll never know."

"It wasn't an in-depth search I conducted last night," she heard herself telling him. God help her, she was flirting again, Lydia realized. But that didn't change any of the words that followed. "There's at least enough left to discuss over dessert."

Amusement lifted the corners of his mouth again. "Are you asking me out?"

Lydia became acutely aware that they were being overheard. Even so, she kept on, trying not to incriminate herself.

Her answer was neither yes nor no. "I'm expanding on your scenario—and asking for cooperation."

He moved aside as the young nurse pushed the crash cart out of the room. "With the scenario?"

"With the situation." Damn it, what was the matter with her? She was supposed to be concentrating on her job, on the man in the bed, not on the tall man in front of her. "Never mind," she said abruptly.

"Forget I said anything." She nodded toward the bed. "Is he going to be all right?"

Experience had taught Lukas to be cautious in his optimism.

"He's stable. For the moment," he qualified. "But I'm going to have to ask you to give me your word that you won't talk to him tonight. And that you won't agitate him when you finally do talk to him."

She didn't like being talked to as if she were slow witted. "I'll bring incense and candles," Lydia retorted.

"And don't growl."

She looked at him sharply, aware of the grin on the orderly's face. "I don't growl."

"You growl," Lukas contradicted. "You're just so intent, you don't hear it."

He glanced over his shoulder at the monitors. Everything looked to be all right. For now, they were out of the woods. But he knew how quickly that could change. So much for catching that program tonight. Maybe the television in the doctors' lounge had been repaired—but he doubted it.

"I'll hang around for a little while," he told the intern. "Call me if he takes a turn for the worse."

The intern dragged his eyes away from the special agent and nodded with enthusiasm.

Taking hold of Lydia's good arm, Lukas ushered her from the room.

Caught off guard, she found herself moving out the door before she could stop him. Lydia saw Rodriguez looking at them oddly, then averting his eyes the instant he realized she saw him.

"What are you doing?" she rasped at Lukas.

He pulled the door closed behind them. "Making sure he doesn't take a turn for the worse."

Lydia pulled her arm away. "Look, his well-being is important to me."

Lukas loomed over her. "No," he contradicted, "it's not. You just want him conscious long enough to get the information you're after."

She wasn't about to get into an argument with Graywolf. It had be a long time since she'd felt the need to justify herself to anyone. "Is that so bad?"

Yes, it was bad. It meant she had no conscience, but that was her problem, not his. "For one thing, that puts you on a collision course with my oath."

She decided that the best way to handle this—and him—was with humor. Otherwise, they were both going to butt heads throughout Conroy's stay at Blair Memorial. "Which oath? The one you took in medical school, or the one I saw you swallowing when you pushed me out of the way."

"The former, and I didn't push you," he corrected her. "I moved you."

"You certainly 'move' hard." Overhearing, Rodriguez raised a brow as he looked in her direction. Pulling Lukas out of Rodriguez's earshot, she stood, studying the physician for a moment. And then she smiled. "Maybe I've changed my mind, Graywolf. Maybe I do like you."

He covered his heart with his hand. "I can die a happy man now."

She snorted. And maybe she'd been too hasty in her reversal, she thought. "Or at least a sarcastic one."

There it was again, he noted. That spark, that fire in her eyes. He found himself intrigued. "Never knew I was one, until yesterday."

Her eyes swept over him. Whether she liked him or not, there was no denying that he was one hell of a good-looking man. Or that there was something about him that pulled at her. Hard. "Never too late to learn things about yourself."

He looked at her, his thoughts taking a deeper, inward turn. "No, maybe not," he agreed quietly.

The word "magnificent" echoed through his brain as he saw Lydia approach him the following evening. The spark he had witnessed in her eyes had evolved into a full-fledged bonfire and there was anger in each step she took that brought her closer to him. It was obvious she'd come looking for him and it wasn't just to ask after his health.

Anger became her, he decided. Even if that anger was directed against him.

"You, Graywolf," Lydia called to him in case he had any ideas about walking away. "You did this on purpose, didn't you?" It wasn't a question. It was an accusation.

He placed the chart he was signing down on the

nurse's desk. Technically, he was through for the night. But not if the look in her eyes had anything to say about it, he thought.

"If you want an answer, you're going to have to be more specific than that."

Did he think he was going to play games with her? That he could just give her what he probably thought was a bone-melting look and she'd forget all about her job? If he did, he had no idea what he was up against, she vowed silently.

"You deliberately placed my prisoner into a drug-induced coma."

She was almost shouting at him and all he could think about was kissing her, silencing her mouth with his own. "Drug-induced comas are deliberate, yes."

His mild tone nearly drove her up the wall. She felt like a child, being patronized.

"Why?" she demanded. "Why did you do that?"

The action had solid medical reasoning behind it. "Because Conroy'll heal faster that way. He's on a ventilator and has got tubes running all through his body. His body can't deal with everything that's going on and still heal, too. This way, it can focus on the healing process."

All this trouble, all this concern, for a man who was a worthless human being. Sometimes the unfairness of it all turned her stomach. She spoke before she could think to stop herself. But she'd had nightmares. She'd been at the mall and this time, it had been her father she'd been unable to save.

"What about Bobby Richards?"

He stopped to think but the name meant nothing to him. "Who?"

"Bobby Richards," she repeated, banking down a wave of emotion. "The boy Conroy's bomb killed." She'd made it her business to find out his name. And to give his parents her sincerest condolences. "Tell me, Doctor, how's he supposed to focus on getting well?"

They were at an impasse. Lukas blew out a breath. "I can't answer that."

"No, neither can I," she told him honestly. "But I'd like to be able to answer the question 'How are you going to be sure Conroy's New World group isn't going to pull this kind of thing again?"

Lukas heard the frustration in her voice. He wished she'd realize that, ultimately, they were on the same team and did have the same goal. He didn't want to see teens come in with their limbs torn up, or their lives prematurely cut short, either.

"Don't you have any other sources? Can't the person who gave you Conroy's name get you the names of the others in the group?" It seemed to him that would be the most logical way to proceed.

She closed her eyes for a minute and shook her head. "No, he can't."

Was she just being too stubborn, like some obsessive dog that had caught hold of something, digging in and refusing to let go? "Why not?"

She opened her eyes again. The image wouldn't

leave. "It's a little hard to talk with your throat slit. We found his body the morning after the bombing."

They'd found him on the floor of his rented motel room, a drying pool of blood encircling his head. The informant had bled to death. "Somebody must have found out he tipped us off."

The informant, Warren Howard, had been a nondescript man whose life had been a series of wrong turns. There'd been no one to mourn over him. So she had. "So, you see, Conroy's our only hope."

So maybe Ms. Special Agent wasn't obsessive, he relented. Maybe she was just doing her job. "He's not going to do you any good dead," he reminded her.

"No," she admitted, trying to come to terms with her frustration, "he's not."

"And he's not coming out of the coma tonight."

She looked at Lukas hopefully. It had been a long, fruitless day, her shoulder ached and she was tired. She needed something to go on, something to hang on to. "Tomorrow?"

"We'll see. Maybe," he augmented, taking pity on her.

Lydia raised her eyes to his, surprised at the softer tone.

He supposed, looking back, that it was her eyes that had gotten to him. Otherwise, he wasn't really sure what his excuse was, or what it was that prompted him to ask, "When do you get off duty?"

She laughed shortly. The work was never really done. "Never."

He knew how that felt. He took his patients home with him each night, in his head, reviewing their cases in the wee hours of the morning when sleep refused to crawl into bed with him.

"How about technically?"

Lydia glanced at her watch. "An hour ago."

He'd just seen his last patient, written his last note for the evening, barring an emergency. "Would you like to have that dessert now?"

Lydia looked at him, confused. For a moment she didn't know what he was talking about. And then she remembered their conversation from the other morning about sharing things over a meal.

A smile found its way to her lips. "Why, are you going to share some things about yourself?"

He'd bet that she was really good at interrogation once she got going. There were things he found himself wanting to learn about her. "Tell you what, we'll make it a drink instead and it can be an equal trade of information."

The question why hovered on her lips, but never crossed from her mind into the region of sound. Instead, Lydia smiled and inclined her head.

"All right, Doctor, you're on."

They exchanged small talk while they waited for the waiter to return with the drinks they'd ordered. Once the glasses were set in front of them and the waiter retreated, they circled one another mentally, both looking for an opening, a weakness to turn to their advantage.

He raised his glass in a toast. "To discovery."

"Discovery," she echoed, then took a long sip of her Screwdriver. She set the glass down. She could almost feel the electricity between them and wondered if he was aware of it, too, and just what it would mean in the long run. "Do I get to go first?"

He nodded. "Ladies usually do."

Chivalry had long been absent from her life. She didn't usually encounter it anymore. "You *are* a throwback."

He didn't consider himself a man who could comfortably live beneath any label. "If you did your research, you'd know that the Navaho tribe is matriarchal."

"A culture of Barbara Stanwycks." The grin that came to her lips was a fond one. "I could identify with that."

The name meant nothing to him. "Who?"

She forgot at times that most people hadn't had the kind of upbringing she had. "A movie star from the forties and fifties," she clarified. "Always played tough, gutsy women making a mark for themselves in a man's world."

He tipped his glass back and let the raw whiskey burn its way slowly down his throat to his stomach. He focused on the sensation and not the fact that he was finding the woman across from him increasingly more attractive, increasingly more desirable. "You watched old movies?"

She nodded. "With my dad. He was a walking encyclopedia of movie trivia. I wanted to please him, so I soaked it up, too." Lydia blinked, suddenly becoming aware of what she'd just said. "You tricked me."

His expression was one of silently protesting innocence. "How?"

"I just gave you two pieces of information." And he hadn't given her any.

Lukas held up his index finger. "Technically, it's one—hyphenated."

She laughed, shaking her head. "You sure you're a doctor and not a lawyer?"

He liked the sound of her laugh. It went straight to his gut and stirred him. Or was that the whiskey? he wondered.

But there hadn't been much of that and there had been a time he could put away a pint and not feel it.

"Where I come from, you have to be a little bit of both, with a few other things thrown in, as well."

She tried to envision him the way he had been as a youth—wild, determined to defy authority. The image pulled her further in.

"Such as?"

"A survivor." His tone was noncommittal. Lukas indicated her glass. "You want a refill?"

She looked down at it. Somehow half of it had disappeared. "I haven't finished this one yet."

He smiled at her over the glass. "I'll wait."

I'll wait. Lydia wrapped both hands around her chunky glass, trying to ignore the very unsettled feeling that had just taken another lunge in her stomach.

Chapter 7

Lydia wasn't accustomed to dealing with nerves, at least, not her own.

It wasn't that she was foolhardy, but for the most part, fear had no place in her life. She wasn't reckless, proceeding through her day with a fair amount of cautious sense, but she never dwelled on what might happen to her, only on what she needed to do. Purpose and duty, that was her focus.

This was different. In every way.

She was sitting across from a man she knew she shouldn't even be near. Because he was dangerous. Not in the typical FBI sense that she was accustomed to dealing with, but dangerous to her.

Personally.

There was something about Lukas Graywolf, something that drew her to him, even though he wasn't the type she was usually attracted to. And never with this intensity. Her instincts told her that interacting with Lukas could and would be different.

If she allowed it to happen.

The problem was, she didn't know whether she should or not.

So then what was she doing here? Exploring?

The truth of it was, she'd gone out for this drink with him on a dare. Her own dare. She'd felt an uneasiness in his presence that was increasingly titillating and had decided to test herself.

Now she wasn't so sure if that was a good idea. Lydia was growing acutely aware of his eyes on her. So blue, even in this light, they made her think of a cloudless sky. And she felt as if they were delving into her very soul.

That would have given him an advantage over her, she thought cryptically.

"So," he was saying after what felt like a long, pregnant pause, "what else should I know about you?"

She regarded her near empty drink rather than look at him. It was called regrouping.

"Seems to me you've had your turn at asking. It's your turn to trade now."

He leaned back, studying her. The warm candlelight made her features that much more sensual. As if the woman needed it, he thought. He wondered if she was even aware of her looks. She certainly didn't act as though she were. He'd known women who were far less attractive than she who'd used their looks like a weapon. Ms. Special Agent seemed oblivious to what the mirror showed her.

"I don't know what it is you know about me already. Maybe if you just ask a question," he suggested, "I'll see if I want to answer."

He was qualifying this. She wasn't surprised. She didn't even blame him. She intended to do the same. "You like your privacy."

"If that's a question, yes." Tilting his glass back, Lukas drained it of the last few amber drops that had mingled with the melting ice.

Lydia couldn't keep her eyes off his hands as he replaced the chunky glass in front of him on the table. They looked to be what they were, a surgeon's hands with long, slender fingers. And yet there was something powerful about them at the same time.

She realized that she was imagining how it would feel to have those same hands stroking her body.

Damn it, she usually had better control over her thoughts than this. What the hell was happening to her discipline?

Lydia cleared her throat, as if that could somehow help clear her mind, as well.

"That was an assumption, actually. I suppose this gives us something in common." She saw him raise a questioning eyebrow. "I like my privacy, too."

Slowly, Lukas stroked the rim of his glass with his thumb, his eyes never leaving her face. "So what are we doing here, playing Twenty Questions when neither one of us likes giving answers?''

She felt her mouth growing dry. ''I'm not really sure.'' As someone determined to be proven fearless, she looked into his eyes. Trying not to allow herself to be drawn into their hypnotic pull. With effort, she reverted to her agent mode, seeking shelter there. ''What *are* you doing here?''

''That's easy.'' He lifted his empty glass in a silent toast. ''Having drinks with a woman I find very stimulating.''

Amusement brushed along her lips. ''Interesting word for a heart surgeon to use.''

''Who better?'' His curiosity about her growing, Lukas decided to see just how willing she actually was to tell him something about herself. ''Do you like what you do, Special Agent? Think carefully now.''

She couldn't decide whether or not he was teasing her by using her title, but she had to admit that she liked the sound of it when he said it. And she didn't have to think carefully, she knew.

''Most of the time. I know I like making a difference.''

There was a ''but'' there she wasn't saying, Lukas thought. Waiting, he finally supplied the prompt himself. ''But?''

''But sometimes I don't.'' That's when the job ate at her. It wasn't the pieces of the puzzle that kept her awake at night, it was the failures. ''Like this last time. We weren't there in time to stop the bombing.''

"But from what I heard, they managed to get most of the people who were there evacuated. Because you called to warn the security guards."

Most, but not all. She shut her eyes. "I guess it could have been worse."

She knew herself very well. She'd never been the type to be satisfied with half a loaf. She wasn't satisfied until she had the keys to the entire bakery in her possession.

Lydia opened her eyes again, looking directly at him, her gaze intense. "But it could have been better. Much better. There could have been no one wounded, no one killed."

He knew she was thinking of that boy. The one whose funeral she'd attended. "Are you including Conroy in that package?"

Her expression sobered and she straightened in her chair. Her voice when she answered was clipped, precise.

"He comes under a different heading." She couldn't gauge what Graywolf was thinking, but she could make a fair guess. "I'm not a cold-blooded woman, Graywolf."

He'd thought that initially, but not anymore. She was far too passionate. "I've already come to that conclusion on my own."

How? a soft voice whispered through her mind. *How did you come to that conclusion?*

She banished the voice, telling herself that it made

no difference to her one way or another what he thought or how he had reached his conclusions.

Still, she found herself wanting to make him understand. "But something inside me freezes when I have to deal with people who kill without thought, who think they are so right that there's no room for argument, for differences." She sounded as if she were preaching, she thought. "I don't hate easily, but I do hate bigots."

Half his life had been spent fighting bigots, struggling out of the box that stereotypical thinking insisted on relegating him to. It had been a hard road from there to here. "I guess that gives us something else in common."

She pushed her empty glass away. "I know something else we have in common."

"Oh?"

"Neither one of us should have too much to drink." It was time to leave, she thought. Before things heated up. "You never know when they might need us."

She was right. Besides, he wanted his head clear tonight. "Doesn't leave much room for a personal life, does it?"

She studied him for a second before replying. "Do you really want one?"

"Why, don't you?"

No, she thought, she didn't. Otherwise, she wouldn't spend as much time on the job as she did. For the most part, her job *was* her life.

"I don't really have any hobbies beyond watching old movies." She couldn't remember when she'd taken more than a couple of days off, and that had been to help out with and attend her mother's wedding. "I'd be bored inside of three hours."

As a kid he'd had too much time on his hands and he knew where that had led him then. But he'd come a long way from that troubled youth. Thanks, in no small part, to his uncle Henry and the boxing club Uncle Henry had established on the reservation. Boxing had given him a purpose, a goal and a place to be that didn't involve getting into trouble. Now Lukas wished he could have just part of that time to do all the things he wanted to do.

"Not me. I've got more than enough to keep me occupied."

She knew all about his volunteer work, and the free surgeries he and his friends performed back on his reservation. But to her, that was all part and parcel of the same thing. To her free time meant something completely different from what occupied your time during working hours.

"Then why choose something that makes such a demand on you?"

He found himself telling her things he didn't normally share. And not minding it.

"Because I like the idea that I can save lives, that because of me Mr. Lindstrom will see his grandchild born and Mrs. Halloway will blow out the candles on her ninety-fifth birthday cake and Jon Erickson will

In Graywolf's Hands

live to graduate from high school this year. Besides, I get to give back a little.''

''Give back?''

He nodded, thinking of the reservation. Of the people who had grown up with the simplest of amenities, thinking this was the way it was supposed to be because they knew nothing else.

''To the people who put themselves out for me when my life didn't look quite as rosy as—'' He stopped, realizing he'd gone a little too far, talked a little too much. ''Hey, now who's the underhanded one?''

She laughed at the accusation. ''Sorry, part of my training, getting people to talk.''

''You're good at it,'' he allowed.

The simple compliment warmed her.

The waiter approached, his body language making his inquiry for him before he had a chance to form the words. She shook her head at the thought of a second drink. She felt intoxicated enough as it was. Which wasn't like her, she thought. She could hold a great deal more than she'd had tonight.

Lydia had an uneasy feeling that sipping a simple drink comprised of vodka and orange juice wasn't what was sending her head spinning this way, but there was no sense in taking any chances. Alcohol would only make the situation worse.

''You're sure?'' Lukas asked.

''I'm sure. It's getting late, anyway. And it wouldn't hurt me to turn in before midnight one night a month.'' She leaned over to pick up the small purse she kept with her.

Rather than try to talk her into having another, Lukas asked the waiter to bring the check. He paid cash and left a generous tip.

''Was that to impress me?''

Graywolf had left more as a tip than the drinks had cost. He didn't strike her as the kind of man who would go out of his way to impress anyone, but she was the first to agree that she wasn't always infallible in her judgment.

''No, that was to help the waiter with his expenses. He's working his way through school. I treated him in the emergency room,'' he added when she looked at him curiously. ''He collided with another waiter and got some nasty cuts from the broken glasses as a result.''

''They have heart surgeons treating lacerations?''

''They do when it's a Sunday night, the E.R. doctor's busy and there's no one else available.''

He held the door open for her and they walked out together. There was a full moon and it was painting everything within reach in shades of pale gold. Lukas looked at her and realized that he didn't want the evening to end. Not yet.

''How far away do you live?''

She thought that a strange question, coming out of the blue. ''About ten miles, why?''

''My place is closer. It's just three miles from here.'' Damn it, he was fumbling, he thought. Like some college kid asking a girl up to his place. He wondered if she'd laugh in his face, but it didn't stop him from asking. "Would you like to come over for a nightcap?"

Self-preservation dictated that she turn him down. Politely or flippantly, but either way, firmly. She'd always known when she was in too deep. It was initially a gift that she had honed to perfection over the years. It had managed to save her more than once from a situation that could have turned deadly.

This wouldn't turn deadly, but it was dangerous nonetheless, just as she had already decided that Lukas was.

But that old determination to see how far she could go in any given situation rose to the fore again, daring her to accept his invitation. Daring her to see if she could resist him and ultimately walk away when the time came to leave. Daring her to explore regions that were unfamiliar to her.

"I don't want another drink," she told him. "Do you have coffee?"

For a second he thought she was turning him down. There had been a hint of relief swirling through him. Relief because maybe he wanted to see her just a little more than he should.

But the relief that came with her acceptance was greater.

"If you like." He tried to recall the contents of his refrigerator and vaguely thought he remembered seeing a carton of juice. "I could probably scare up some orange juice if you have a mind to be healthy."

"All right," she allowed, "you're on. Provided neither of our pagers goes off."

"Understood." He led the way into the parking lot. Because it had been fairly crowded when they'd arrived, they had been forced to park in different rows. "Wait here," Lukas told her. "I'll swing around to pick you up."

Lydia nodded and unlocked her car. Sliding in behind the steering wheel, she told herself she had precisely three minutes to do the smart thing and get the hell out of here. Her job tested her enough every day. She didn't need to prove anything more to herself. There was certainly no reason to play Russian roulette with Graywolf this way.

But when his dark blue sedan pulled into her row, Lydia was still sitting where she was, mentally listing pros and cons for doing what she was doing. She'd never been a coward before, she thought, nodding at him. She wasn't about to start being one on a Friday night in late September.

Lydia started up her car and followed the blue sedan out of the lot and into the flow of traffic.

"I thought all heart surgeons were rich." She turned to look at Lukas as he pocketed the key to his third-floor apartment.

Lukas closed the door behind her, locking it. "You mean, why don't I live in a house?" He smiled. His mother asked the same thing, except that she wanted the house to be in Arizona, near her. "There's only me and I'm not around that much. What do I need with a house? This place more than suits my needs. Can I take your jacket?" he offered.

She hesitated, then nodded. "Sure."

When she began to shrug out of it, he moved around behind her to help her. As he slid the sleeves from her arms, she felt something suspiciously like an electrical shock shoot up both limbs. A little voice advised her to run. She ignored it.

"Thanks," she murmured.

He paused, her jacket draped over his arm, humor curving his generous mouth. "I'm not up on my special agent etiquette. Should I ask you for your gun and holster, too?"

"Never ask an FBI special agent for her weapon," she advised him with a smile. "Unless you want the business end of it first."

Removing her holster, she wrapped the belt around it, then placed it on the kitchen counter.

Hanging her jacket on the coatrack, Lukas eyed the weapon. "Well, that'll certainly keep me on my toes. Isn't it uncomfortable, wearing that?"

"I've gotten used to it." These days, it almost felt strange being without it. "Besides—" she thought of the split-second, life-or-death situation she'd been faced with when Conroy had turned his gun on Elliot "—it comes in handy."

"I imagine in your line of work it does." Checking

the thermostat, he pressed the keypad. The unit began to rumble as it worked its way up to turning over. "How good are you with that thing?"

Her grandfather had taken her to a target range when she was fifteen. It had become a ritual every Saturday morning for the next three years. She could hit a bull's-eye at a remarkable distance. He called her his Annie Oakley. "I generally hit what I aim for."

"I'll keep that in mind." Lukas crossed to his kitchen. "So, what can I get you?"

She thought back to his offer when they left the restaurant. "Orange juice would be nice."

Moving around the small family room, taking in bits and pieces, she stopped before a collection of framed photographs on the wall—black-and-white and color shots freezing scenes of poverty and groups of dark-haired children with bright, shiny smiles. That had to be home. She tried to pick him out.

Opening the refrigerator, Lukas found the carton on the first shelf. He took it out to read the date stamped along the top, then looked at her. "How do you feel about expiration dates?"

"You're going to have to give me a little more than that to work with."

He raised the carton to underscore his question. "The orange juice stopped being good yesterday."

She shrugged. Drinking orange juice one day past its expiration date was far from the most daring thing she'd ever done. Lydia crossed to him.

"I'll take my chances. If I get sick, luckily there's a doctor in the house." She moved behind him and looked into the interior of his refrigerator for herself. The shelves were almost empty. "I take it that shopping for food isn't high on your priority list."

He let the door close. "I usually get something in the cafeteria."

"But not the coffee," she guessed, opening the cupboard, looking for a glass. She found six cans of coffee instead. Nothing fancy, she noted.

"No, not the coffee. I'm particular about that and I need at least two cups to kick start my day." He watched her, amused, as she opened the pantry. "There are more closets in the bedroom."

She'd located a glass on her second try, but had decided to continue taking inventory. No wonder the man looked so fit and lean. There was no junk food around to tempt him.

What did tempt him? she wondered.

She realized that he'd said something to her and was waiting for some sort of response. She played back his words in her head and then looked at him over her shoulder. That definitely came under the heading of sarcasm, she thought.

"Excuse me?"

"You look like you're enjoying yourself. I just thought you'd like to look in the closets I've got in the bedroom." He gestured to the small hallway and the two rooms that lay beyond. "I have to warn you, though, there's not much in the way of a wardrobe. I tend to live in jeans and work shirts when I'm not in scrubs or a lab coat.''

She let the doors fall. They folded into place. ''Sorry, occupational habit. You can learn a lot about a person by what's in their closets. That includes the pantry,'' she added.

He poured a glass of orange juice for her. ''And what did mine tell you?''

She took the glass as he replaced the carton in the refrigerator. Lydia wondered how long he kept things before he threw them out. ''That you're a minimalist and that for a man, you're very neat.''

She had a strange way of wording things, he thought. His eyes slowly washed over her face.

''Does that mean if I were a woman, you'd consider me messy?''

Her heart was inching its way up her throat. She was having much more trouble catching her breath than she had a few minutes ago, when she'd been alone in her car. ''If you were a woman, I would consider it a waste.''

He took the glass of orange juice from her hand and placed it on the counter. Even from where he was standing he could feel the heat, the pull that had been haunting him ever since he'd first laid eyes on her. He moved a little closer to the fire.

Slowly he combed his fingers through her hair, clearing it away from her face. ''I'd say that puts us in agreement again.''

She hardly heard the words, even though she was concentrating on making them out. But it was hard to hear anything with her blood rushing in her ears the way it was.

Chapter 8

Like someone snatching a life preserver tossed to them at the last possible moment as they bobbed up and down in a tempestuous sea that was about to swallow them up whole, Lydia turned her head away from Lukas. One more second and she knew he was going to kiss her. Knew she was going to be lost if he did.

That wasn't what she wanted to happen.

Wasn't it?

Wasn't that why she'd agreed to go out and have a drink with him? To come here with him? Because some part of her was curious? Curious to see if this intense attraction that shimmered between them was really all glitter and no substance—like the elaborate facades that were used to create an illusion on a movie studio backlot, all front, no sides, no back, no interior.

She was afraid to find out that there wasn't anything more.

She was afraid to find out that there was.

With his hands on either side of her face, Lukas gently turned her head until she looked at him again. His eyes held her more prisoner than his hands. Hypnotized, she watched as he lowered his mouth to hers.

Determined to remain impervious to whatever was coming next, Lydia still felt her eyes closing and her pulse racing in wild anticipation.

She didn't even come close to impervious.

Lights exploded in her head, raining down and bathing her in instant, intense heat, leaving no part untouched. Willing herself to remain still, to somehow maintain distance, did nothing. She wasn't listening.

Lydia rose up on her toes, leaning into him, wrapping her arms around his neck.

And surrendering.

The hunger came full-blown and immediate, surprising him. Lukas was accustomed to exercising extreme control over himself, holding unwanted, complicating feelings at such distances that they never became even a remote threat to his way of life.

That wasn't happening here.

Fissures ripped through his control, cracking it at a mind-numbing speed. Rather than remaining off to the sideline, feelings assaulted him from all sides.

An Important Message from the Editors

Dear Reader,

Because you've chosen to read one of our fine romance novels, we'd like to say "thank you!" And, as a special way to thank you, we've selected two more of the books you love so well, plus an exciting Mystery Gift, to send you absolutely FREE!

Please enjoy them with our compliments...

Pam Powers

P.S. And because we value our customers, we've attached something extra inside...

Peel off seal and Place inside...

EDITOR'S FREE GIFT SEAL · THANK YOU

How to validate your Editor's
FREE GIFT
"Thank You"

1. Peel off gift seal from front cover. Place it in space provided at right. This automatically entitles you to receive 2 FREE BOOKS and a fabulous mystery gift.

2. Send back this card and you'll get 2 brand-new Silhouette Intimate Moments® novels. These books have a cover price of $4.50 each in the U.S. and $5.25 each in Canada, but they are yours to keep absolutely free.

3. There's no catch. You're under no obligation to buy anything. We charge nothing—ZERO—for your first shipment. And you don't have to make any minimum number of purchases—not even one!

4. The fact is, thousands of readers enjoy receiving their books by mail from the Silhouette Reader Service™. They enjoy the convenience of home delivery...they like getting the best new novels at discount prices BEFORE they're available in stores...and they love their *Heart to Heart* subscriber newsletter featuring author news, horoscopes, recipes, book reviews and much more!

5. We hope that after receiving your free books you'll want to remain a subscriber. But the choice is yours— to continue or cancel, any time at all! So why not take us up on our invitation, with no risk of any kind. You'll be glad you did!

6. Don't forget to detach your FREE BOOKMARK. And remember...just for validating your Editor's Free Gift Offer, we'll send you THREE gifts, *ABSOLUTELY FREE!*

GET A
FREE MYSTERY GIFT...

SURPRISE MYSTERY GIFT
*COULD BE YOURS **FREE** AS*
A SPECIAL "THANK YOU" FROM
THE EDITORS OF SILHOUETTE

Visit us online at
www.eHarlequin.com

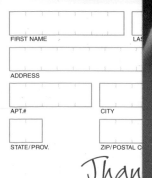

The Silhouette Reader Service™ — Here's how it works:

BUSINESS REPLY MAIL
FIRST-CLASS MAIL   PERMIT NO. 717-003   BUFFALO, NY

POSTAGE WILL BE PAID BY ADDRESSEE

SILHOUETTE READER SERVICE
3010 WALDEN AVE
PO BOX 1867
BUFFALO NY 14240-9952

NO POSTAGE
NECESSARY
IF MAILED
IN THE
UNITED STATES

His mouth slanted over hers, taking, giving, reveling in the taste, the feel, of her. Reveling in the excitement that was throbbing all through his body. Her scent, her flavor, was filling every part of him, his head, his senses, his entire being.

And yet he couldn't get enough of her. He wanted more, craved more.

Needed more.

As if they were separate entities, governed only by instincts, his hands skimmed over her, caressing, possessing. Peeling away her garments.

When he relived it later, Lukas wasn't aware of actually undressing her, only of getting closer to what his passions desired.

Lydia moved with each pass of his hand, shrugging out of her cumbersome clothing, divesting him of his. She found herself desperate to get rid of the layers that encompassed his body, keeping it from her.

The closer she came, the more excited she grew, trembling in anticipation of his hands on her naked body and hers on his.

She wanted to touch him. To have him touch her. To waken parts of her that had been dormant for so long, she'd given them up for dead. Making love with someone had always been less than satisfying for her. In the end it was always far more disappointing than exhilarating.

This time she knew the expectations were far greater than ever before. If disappointment came, she knew it would be that much more devastating. The smart thing would be to stop now, while she still could.

But she couldn't.

Because she wanted so much.

Impatience goaded her as she pulled at his jeans. Anticipation tantalized her as she felt him tug away her underwear.

With the last of the clothing gone, she pressed her body to his, glorying in the hardness that she felt against her.

It took her breath away.

And yet, it wasn't his body that caused this all-consuming hunger within her. There was something more, something about the man himself.

Her head was spinning.

She was only vaguely aware that he had lowered her to the floor and that she was twisting beneath him, seeking the heat of his body until it was pressed against hers, hard, demanding.

She moaned as his mouth found hers again. The intimate contact sent her pulse soaring. She pulled him closer to her.

It was like walking into the center of a raging bonfire. Willingly.

What was happening consumed her, burned away the layers of self-preservation that had always cocooned her and exposed the very vulnerable, very tender center that she had always tried to protect.

Where her heart lived.

Lukas could feel his blood rushing through his

body, could feel the need slamming through him with the force of a sledgehammer, begging for the final release.

And yet he held off as long as he could, wanting to savor his trip through this uncharted territory, wanting to pleasure her almost more than he wanted to enjoy that pleasure himself.

Damn, what was happening to him? What was she doing to him?

He had no answer, he just didn't want it to stop.

It wasn't enough to explore her body with his hands, Lukas felt the need to taste each part, as well, to sample the flavors there.

Slowly, his breath tantalizing her flesh, he trailed his lips and tongue along the outline of her breasts, the hardened peaks of her nipples, the tempting dip of her quivering belly.

He heard her breathing dissolve into quick, hard gasps as she moaned his name, reaching for him. Gratified, enthused, he kept on tantalizing her even though he felt as if at any moment, he would self-destruct.

His mouth moved lower, suckling, teasing, until Lukas reach her very core. He heard Lydia catch her breath, felt her stiffen as he drove his tongue into the most sensitive part of her.

Hot ice rained over her, blotting out everything as Lydia tried to grasp hold of something with which to anchor herself. There was nothing. Nothing but this overwhelming sensation.

Building.

An explosion racked her body as the sweet agony of a climax came to her.

Exhausted, she fell back, only now realizing that she had raised herself up on her elbows, the better to absorb the sensation.

A second assault came in the wake of the first, creating waves, making things happen to her she would have sworn weren't possible.

Groaning, panting, she felt herself sinking into the carpet.

"It's a federal offense to kill a special agent," she gasped.

The next moment, she realized that she was looking into his face. He had pulled himself up, snaking along her body until he was over her, his hard torso poised above hers.

"Killing you isn't what I have in mind." His breath undulated along her skin, caressing her.

With her last ounce of strength, she framed his face with her hands and pulled his mouth down to hers, kissing him hard.

She arched her body against his, her flesh calling to his.

He slid into her then, wanting to move slowly, finding he had no say in the matter.

Sheathed within her, Lukas began to move urgently, knowing that the time for hanging back was long since gone. He was no more in control of the situation than she was.

Lydia would have readily testified before the highest court that she had no energy left within her, yet somehow she matched him, moving as urgently, as swiftly, as he. Wanting the same goal.

Wanting more than anything to reduce him to the same quivering mass of flesh to which he had reduced her.

The climax that overtook him was hard, prolonged, and sapped every single ounce of his strength.

With his heart pounding, vibrating throughout every inch of his body, Lukas finally sank down against her. He tried to move off to the side to keep from crushing her, but he wasn't sure if he was able to.

Even so, he wanted her again. He couldn't help wondering if this was somehow tied up to some subconscious death wish.

"So, was it good for you?" she whispered against his ear, trying very hard to sound at least a little flippant. There was no way she wanted him to know just how greatly affected she was.

"Good?" She felt his mouth curve against her cheek in a smile. Something stirred within her belly. And within her loins. "I don't think they've invented the word to describe what just happened here."

Because his pride demanded it, Lukas raised himself up on one elbow. It was about all he could manage for the moment.

Her lips were smudged with the imprint of his mouth, and her eyes seemed slightly unfocused as she looked up at him. He realized that Ms. Special Agent was as devastated by what had taken place here as he had been. Good. He would have hated to think that he'd been the only one flattened here tonight.

Lukas shifted a little to the right. "Am I hurting you?"

Lydia slowly moved her head from side to side. There was no question that she was completely exhausted. And yet, something distant within her was asking for it to happen all over again.

More than that, she wanted to curl her body against Lukas and just take comfort in his presence. As if they were two lovers instead of just two people who had given in to a consuming physical need.

The desire to curl up against him carried implications that were far more intimate than what had just occurred here.

It scared her.

"I'm not sure I'd know it if you were," she told him. "My body's numb."

Lukas shifted again, this time more languidly. He began to trail his fingers over her belly and watched as it quivered in response. If that was numb, then he was a Texas Longhorn.

He grinned at her. "You might want to get a second opinion on that."

She was feeling things again. Deep-seated hunger began to rise. How was that possible? She didn't have enough strength to be poured into a shot glass and yet he was stirring her again. Making her want him again.

This was insane.

She had to get out of here before she made a complete fool of herself. Lydia began to sit up, her intent to leave clear, but Lukas laid a gentling hand on her shoulder.

His eyes were beginning the process all over again. The one that held her in place.

"You don't have to be anywhere yet, do you?" he asked quietly.

She wanted to lie, to tell him that she had things to do, calls to make. An entire computer database to search through.

But all she could say was, "No."

There was no triumph in his voice, only satisfaction. "Good, neither do I."

Inclining his head, Lukas kissed her softly, touching only his lips to hers.

Knowing what lay ahead, she dissolved just as swiftly.

And then she felt his smile against her mouth. Lydia pulled her head back, looking at him sharply. Was he laughing at her?

But the smile was kind, gentle. Utterly disarming. He cupped her cheek with his hand, his eyes delving into hers. Touching her soul. "What do you say that this time, we go slowly?"

They'd hardly begun and already her breath was growing short, eluding her. Slow would be a very good way to go. Slow, so that she could savor every moment, every nuance.

Even so, she felt an urgency beginning to build and it was going to be a challenge to hold it in check. She didn't want to be the one who seemed eager here.

"We seem to be in agreement again."

He smiled into her eyes. "Good."

And then, Lukas brought his mouth down to hers and made the rest of the room fade into oblivion.

She never slept more than a few hours at a time anymore. It was because she never knew when she'd have to bounce up, alert and ready to go. She called them catnaps and made the most of them, training herself to feel refreshed whenever she woke up. It was a case of mind over matter.

When she opened her eyes, night still littered the corners of the room. It took her only a moment to orient herself. She was in Lukas's living room. They'd fallen asleep on the floor, she realized, too exhausted to summon the strength even to make it to his bedroom.

The heavy weight she felt sealing her in place was his arm. It was draped across her chest, not possessively so much as protectively.

She tried not to dwell on that.

God, what had she been thinking, letting this happen? She moved her head, looking around, trying to find out a shape that would turn out to be her clothes.

Where were they? She hadn't exactly been giving them her full attention when he'd undressed her.

This wasn't like her. She should have left hours ago, Lydia upbraided herself.

She didn't want to be here when he woke up. She hadn't the foggiest idea what to say to him. Holding her breath, she eased herself out from beneath his arm. The light hair on his arm tickled her skin, sensitizing it as she wiggled free. She could feel goose bumps forming.

Probably just the cold, she told herself. Rising to her knees, she wondered if her legs were going to be able to support her once she tried to stand. Taking no chances, she braced her hand against the edge of the sofa and slowly rose. Her legs felt like day old Jell-O.

Damn, what had happened to her last night? she wondered, her annoyance growing. And why had she let it happen?

Simple, because she'd had no say in the matter. It was like standing in the path of a storm. Lydia felt as if she'd been broadsided by a force far greater than anything she'd ever encountered.

She didn't like the fact that she'd succumbed so completely. It tarnished her own self-image. She was supposed to be bigger than that, stronger than that. After all, he was just a man.

Granted, he was better-looking than most, more exciting in a sexy, turn-of-the-last-century kind of way, but that wasn't supposed to matter to her. She was an

FBI special agent, for God's sake. That was supposed to mean something, wasn't it?

It was supposed to mean that she didn't turn into a plate of mush because some heart-throb heart surgeon kissed her.

She spotted her clothes strewn all over the floor next to the coffee table.

The sooner she got out of here, she told herself, scooping up her bra and blouse, the better.

"Planning to sneak off?"

She spun around, startled, holding the clothes she'd gathered against her. Lukas was propped up on one elbow, looking at her. She blew out a shaky breath, grasping at bravado.

"You're lucky I didn't have a gun on me."

His eyes swept over her very slowly, making her warm. She could literally feel them as they traveled down the length of her body. Could feel his smile as he asked, "Where would you keep it?"

"That's not the point," she retorted. Seeing her skirt, she added it to the pile she held against her. Lydia was more than a little aware of the fact that aside from the clothing she was trying to hold against her, she was completely nude. "You're not supposed to surprise an FBI special agent."

"Why not?" he asked mildly. "The FBI special agent surprised me."

What was that supposed to mean? She was ready for a fight. *Wanted* a fight. Anything that would make her feel in control again.

"Why? Didn't you think I was human?"

"I knew you were human, just not *that* human."
Waiting for some kind of crack, she saw him run his
tongue along his teeth instead.

"What are you doing?"

"Checking to see if any of my teeth are loose."
He pretended to test the soundness with his thumb
and forefinger. "I'm surprised we didn't create some
kind of vortex last night. It got pretty intense at one
point." *At all points,* he thought. If someone had told
him the earth moved, he wouldn't have disputed it.

But he still didn't know how he felt about that. Or
how he wanted to feel.

Lukas rose, completely unselfconscious in his na-
kedness. He nodded toward the kitchen. "Want some
hot coffee?"

What she wanted was hot, all right, but it didn't
have anything to do with coffee. He was testing her,
she thought. Well, damn it, she could pass. She could
handle any test sent her way. Her eyes never leaving
his, she raised her chin defiantly.

"Coffee sounds good." With deliberate noncha-
lance, she picked up her underwear and tucked it beneath the skirt she was holding. "Mind if I shower
first?"

His jeans in his hand, he turned to look at her. He
found himself wanting to join in. But saying so left
him open to too much. So instead he shrugged into
his jeans, foregoing the briefs that were at his feet.
"Go right ahead."

She was staring, she realized. In danger of swallowing her tongue if she formed an answer, Lydia settled for nodding her head and went off to take her shower. A cold one.

Chapter 9

Her hair was damp and curling with riotous carelessness around her face as she came down the hall less than fifteen minutes later. She didn't look like an FBI special agent, but some kind of golden-haired sprite he vaguely recalled his mother telling him about when he was a child and had needed to be lulled to sleep.

The coffeemaker stopped making gurgling sounds. The coffee was ready. Lukas moved two mugs into position and filled each. "You're fast."

"Another occupational habit."

Part of her had debated leaving without even coming into the kitchen. But that would have been cowardly and she didn't tolerate cowardice, least of all her own. Especially since she had no idea what there was to be cowardly about.

She accepted the large mug he placed into her hands like a sacred vessel containing life-giving liquid. "Thanks."

Holding on to the mug with both hands, Lydia drank deeply, letting the hot, steamy liquid unfurl within her. Hoping it would burn away everything in its path and force her to focus her attention on the heat it generated and nothing else.

Like him.

Like the night they'd spent together.

Her body still felt as if it was vibrating from his touch.

The sigh that escaped her lips as she put the mug on the counter was part contented, part edgy.

Hearing it, Lukas smiled, remembering that the same sound had echoed in the air last night.

So where did they go from here? he wondered. Did they pretend last night hadn't happened, or act as if it was just a casual encounter that had momentarily heated up?

Had it been a casual encounter? He didn't know. He knew he would rather it had been, because that would have meant no complications, but he just wasn't sure.

Right now, his world looked as if it was in jeopardy of being upended and he had no idea how he actually felt about that.

Lukas retreated to safer ground. "Want any breakfast?"

"No, I—"

Sudden rhythmic beeps had her looking down at the pager at her waist. It had taken some doing to locate the device this morning after her shower. Somehow, it had managed to get itself kicked under the sofa.

She recognized the number. It was Elliot's. Why wasn't he calling her on the cell phone?

"I have to make a call," she told Lukas as she reached into her pocket.

Lukas started to nod when he heard his own pager go off. "Looks like we're both in demand this morning."

Lukas couldn't help being relieved that they wouldn't be faced with making small talk over mugs of cooling coffee. He wasn't sure just what he would have said. For the first time in years he felt uncertain about a situation.

The number belonged to the hospital rather than the answering service that took his office calls after hours. Lukas picked up the receiver from the wall phone and pressed the second speed dial button. Cradling the receiver against his neck and ear, he turned to watch Lydia. She had her back to him, her voice low as she spoke on her cell phone. There was a small, zigzag damp spot on her back where her towel hadn't reached.

He wondered what she would have said if he'd followed his first impulse and gotten into the shower with her.

The object wouldn't have been water conservation.

He'd wanted to make love to her again. Still wanted to. Last night had been like nothing he could ever remember. So much so that he was beginning to doubt his own memory. Further exploration would be called for if he was ever to have any peace of mind.

He heard someone pick up on the other end. "This is Dr. Graywolf, you paged me?"

"Hi, Dr. Graywolf, this is Wanda," the cheery voice was laced with familiarity. "Sorry to bother you so early but we've got a patient who walked in here and he insists on seeing you."

Her back still to him, Lydia was bending to pick up the pen she'd just dropped. He watched her skirt ride up the back of her legs and felt something tightening in his gut. Definitely hadn't gotten his fill last night, he thought.

"What's this patient's name?"

"That's just it, Doctor," the woman told him, "the man won't give us one. But he refuses to see anyone else except you. Said you would understand once you got here."

"'He,'" Lukas repeated, trying to think of someone he knew who would want to play games like this. But no one came to mind. None of his patients were shy about their identities. This didn't make sense. "What does this 'he' look like?"

"Well, that's the funny thing. He looks a little like you, except a lot older." There was an embarrassed pause. "I mean…"

Wanda was obviously stumbling over her own

tongue. She'd been practically the first person he'd met when he'd come to work in the E.R. and he was fond of the older woman. Lukas put her out of her misery.

"I'll be there in twenty minutes. If this mystery patient's suffering any immediate discomfort, have Dr. Reynolds take a look at him," he instructed. A senior cardiac surgeon, Wyatt Reynolds lived across the street from the hospital. Since his wife's untimely passing six years ago, he made himself almost constantly available for any medical emergencies at the hospital if there was no one on duty to take over.

"You got it," Wanda promised. "See you in twenty minutes."

Lukas replaced the receiver just as Lydia turned around, flipping her cell phone closed. Her cheeks were flushed and there was excitement in her eyes. It was different than the kind he'd witnessed last night.

"Good news?" he guessed.

She nodded, tucking the cell phone into her pocket. "I've got to run. My partner thinks we might have a lead on one of the other bombers." She nodded at his pager. "What about you?"

He began to button his shirt. "Somebody came into the E.R. asking for me."

She dragged her eyes away from his chest. The open shirt had been a definite distraction. "A patient?"

Without a name to go by, Lukas couldn't speak for his past association with the man. "In all likelihood, he will be.'' He could postpone his shower until later, he decided, once he met with the mystery patient. If things got too hectic and he didn't have a chance to get back, he could always use the facilities at the hospital. ''Can I give you anything to go?''

Yes, an encore of last night. The response leaped into her mind out of nowhere. Lydia felt her cheeks growing warm a moment before she blocked out the feeling. She didn't know if he'd seen the telltale color.

Lydia tried to distract him. ''You have any of those quickie pastries you pop into a toaster? You know the kind I mean, sugar, fat and tinfoil.''

''You just named my top three food groups, after coffee.'' He opened the freezer and pushed a few boxes around. He had three choices to offer her. ''Strawberry, blueberry or apple cinnamon?''

She crossed to the refrigerator and stood behind him. ''I love apple cinnamon.''

''Apple cinnamon it is.''

Lukas plucked one out of the box. He didn't bother saying that she'd selected his favorite, or that she was taking the last one. The less talk between them right now, he decided, the better. He needed to sort a few things out and to put them in their proper perspective. He couldn't seem to do that right now. Probably because the memory of last night was too fresh in his mind and because she smelled of his shampoo and his soap and something within him was turning alarmingly and strangely possessive.

All he could think about was kissing her again.

Making love with her again.

She was peeling away the foil, making her way to the door. "Don't you want to toast it?" he asked.

"No time." She took a small bite. "I'll see you at the hospital," she promised.

He hadn't thought about the next time he would see her. "What?"

Her parting comment seemed to surprise him, she realized. Did he think she was just going to cease existing the moment she stepped outside his apartment? "Conroy's got to wake up sometime—unless you plan to keep him permanently doped up."

"No plans," he told her. "See you later."

Almost out the door, Lydia hesitated, then doubled back, took hold of the front of his shirt and pulled him toward her. In a movement that, to varying degrees, took them both by surprise, she planted a quick, intense kiss on his mouth.

"See ya," she repeated, releasing his shirt.

She was gone in a heartbeat. His. His heart slammed against his rib cage at the same time the front door slammed against the doorjamb.

He had absolutely no idea what to make of that. Or her.

But he had someplace to be and no time to waste trying to figure out the actions of one diminutive, mercurial special agent.

Or himself for that matter.

Lukas poured a glass of orange juice and gulped it down on his way to the front door. One of his shirt-

tails was still sticking out as he got into his car. But
then, neatness only counted as far as the stitches he
made when working on a patient.

Catching all but one of the lights and managing to
squeak through that one, Lukas made it to the hospital
in under the promised twenty minutes. The day felt
more like spring than fall. The sun was warm early
and the sky was an incredible shade of blue. There
was no sign of the rain that had hit previously. All it
all, it felt like a glorious day to be alive.

For once, the emergency room parking lot was almost empty. He left his car in the last space right
beside the wall and hurried in through the electronic
doors.

Lukas nodded absently at an orderly he recognized
by sight if not by name and went directly to the admitting area. The young woman sitting at the desk
was unfamiliar to him. Hospital personnel changed
only slightly less frequently than the tides. He flipped
his name tag around so that she could see it.

"I'm Dr. Graywolf. There's a patient here asking
for me."

From her expression, the woman didn't appear to
know what or who he was talking about. Turning in
her chair, she called out to the heavy-set woman next
to the coffeemaker. "Wanda?"

Wanda Monroe, as dark as the coffee she favored,
came forward, a big, bright smile on her lips as she
saw Lukas. More than two decades his senior, Wanda

treated him the way she treated most of the young doctors at the hospital, as if he were part of her extended family.

"What did you do, Doctor, fly?"

"Caught all the lights," he replied.

"Must have." She set down her spoon and crossed to the desk with a mug of very strong coffee. "Sorry to get you in before your hours, Dr. Graywolf, but he insisted on seeing you. Won't let anyone else near him. Said it had to be you or nobody." Wanda's dark eyes swept over him. "Guess you've got the magic touch, Doctor." Her laugh was deep and completely infectious. "Maybe someday I'll find out for myself if you do or not."

"What would your husband say?"

"Probably, 'pass the remote, honey.'" She winked at him. "As long as we don't televise it, Ed won't know a thing about it," she chuckled, her dark eyes dancing. She indicated the area behind her. "Patient's waiting for you in Room Six."

He nodded his thanks and went back to the rear of the hospital. Room Six was to his left.

He stopped dead just inside the swinging door.

It had to be a joke, he realized, coming forward. One his mother had to be in on, since she was the one who had told him about the bogus fishing trip.

"Uncle Henry, what are you doing here? Why didn't you just come to my apartment?" Genuinely happy to see the man he freely credited with saving

him from sure self-destruction, Lukas embraced his
uncle, enveloping him in a bear hug.

Henry Spotted Owl returned the hug with a great
deal of feeling, hanging on to Lukas for a long moment.

The hug felt almost anemic compared to what Lukas was accustomed to from to his uncle. Something
was wrong. He stepped back. His pleasure at the surprise visit died away as he took another, more focused
look at his uncle.

Lukas saw that the beloved leathery face, which
bore the scars of hard living, looked somewhat pale.
The last time he had seen Henry was six months ago.
The man had looked robust, as fit as the day he had
taken Lukas under his wing at the boxing club he'd
started more than fifteen years ago.

The word "robust" was not the first one that came
to mind now.

He still wasn't getting the full picture. Lukas sat
on the edge of the gurney beside his uncle, placing
his arm around the older man's shoulders. When had
they gotten to feel so frail? Or had he just been too
busy to notice?

"What happened to the fishing trip? I talked to
Mother yesterday and she said you were going away
on a fishing trip."

Henry shrugged uncomfortably. "I didn't want her
to know I was coming here. I didn't want to worry
her. I figured if she thought I was going fishing, she

wouldn't riddle me with questions about something I don't want to talk about.''

The picture was beginning to take shape. And Lukas couldn't say that he particularly liked what he was seeing. "But you'll talk to me about it?''

"You're the doctor.''

Lukas remembered other times when they had sat just like this, side by side on a bed in his closet-size bedroom back on the reservation. Then it had been his uncle who was the man with the wisdom. He didn't know if he was comfortable with this reversal.

"Do you need one?''

Henry Spotted Owl frowned. He wanted to say no, that he didn't. That he was as healthy now as the day he'd walked into his sister's house to tame his wild nephew and to make sure they remained a family in every sense of the word. But that would have been a lie. And he wasn't here to lie.

"It's getting to look that way,'' he told his nephew with a studied casualness that the expression on his face couldn't quite pull off.

There was pride involved here and Lukas knew he had to proceed cautiously to spare his uncle. "Doc Brown send you here?''

Henry laughed harshly. "Doc Brown doesn't know his scalpel from his stethoscope.''

Lukas doubted that his uncle would have sought him out in a professional capacity if someone hadn't started him thinking along those lines. His uncle was a fiercely proud, fiercely private man, and asking for help wasn't something he did easily. "Exactly what did Doc Brown say that made you come here?"

There was smoldering anger in the dark eyes as Henry raised them to look at his nephew. "That he doesn't think I'll live to be a hundred."

Since Henry had come to him, there was only one logical conclusion to be drawn. "Your heart?"

Henry nodded. "He thinks I need bypass surgery."

Lukas remembered Doc Brown. The man represented the only medical care available on the reservation until Lukas and his friends had taken to making their semi-annual pilgrimages there. Everyone was certain that Doc Brown had been born old and stoop-shouldered. His idea of practicing medicine was to place a Band-Aid strip over a wound and to browbeat patients into rallying. Lukas knew that the old man wouldn't have bandied about the term "bypass surgery" if he wasn't significantly alarmed.

"What kind of a test did he give you?"

There had been several. The names were all foreign to Henry.

"Made me run with these white round little things glued to my chest until I thought my eyes were going to pop out," Henry informed him moodily.

"A treadmill test." That stood to reason, Lukas thought. "What else?"

Henry shrugged. "Took enough blood out of me to make three vampires happy. Don't remember what else."

"That's okay. Do you have any of the test results with you?"

Henry looked annoyed as he shook his head. "I didn't want to tell him where I was going, either. Man's got a mouth like an old woman, always talking. Nobody's business but mine."

"No problem, I can have him fax the reports over." The last time he'd been on the reservation, he'd brought a fax machine and a renovated computer with him, making the man a gift of them both. Doc Brown had grumbled about progress moving too fast for him.

Lukas thought for a long moment, mentally reviewing the cardiac surgeons on staff. He wanted the best for his uncle.

"Thom Harris is an excellent surgeon." The man had a full calendar. "I'm sure I can get you in to see him."

"Why would I want to see him?" The question was belligerent.

"A consultation is standard before surgery." Henry's finances were tight and Lukas worded this as delicately as he could. "Don't worry about his fee, I'll work something out with him."

"There's not going to be a fee," Henry told him. "Because he's not going to operate on me."

Lukas sighed. This was going to be trickier than he thought. He was beginning to realize that what his uncle had come for was to be assured that he didn't need surgery. "Look, Uncle Henry, I know how you feel. And maybe Doc Brown's wrong, maybe you don't need surgery. But if you do, I want you to have the best.''

"So do I, that's why I came here.'' Henry looked at his nephew, seeing for a moment the scared, defiant, fatherless boy who had given his mother so much grief as he had tried to find a meaning in life amid the poverty that surrounded him. "Doc Brown's not wrong. I haven't felt right for a while now. I already know I need the surgery.'' He looked at his nephew. "I want you to be the one to do it.''

He'd gotten so caught up in wording everything just right and saving his uncle's pride that he hadn't seen this coming. But he should have.

"Uncle Henry, I can't operate on you. I'd be too emotionally involved.''

The protest made no sense to the older man. "Of course you'd be emotionally involved. You love me, boy. I want someone who loves me holding that knife, making those cuts.'' He caught hold of Lukas's arm to emphasize his point. "Because someone who loves me has a high stake in my making it through the surgery.''

Rather than shrug out of the hold, Lukas gently placed his hand on top of his uncle's. "Any surgeon who agrees to do the surgery has a high stake in the outcome. And there are rules, Uncle Henry—''

"The hell with rules,'' Henry interrupted. "They've been bent before. Bend them again. You, I want you to do the surgery.'' He pulled himself up, a proud, small bull of a man who had lived life hard and enjoyed every moment he had wrenched away from a less than kind fate. "It's you, Lukas, or I go back to the reservation and go on that fishing trip I told your mother I was taking. Whether I make it back or not..." His voice trailed off as he shrugged.

Lukas sighed. He knew he was cornered. There was no way he was letting his uncle go back without conducting a thorough examination. And if the fears of the reservation doctor were correct, he couldn't allow his uncle to leave without having the surgery. Maybe, under the circumstances, he could bend the rules the way his uncle demanded. Or at least be allowed to assist in the surgery. "You always were a stubborn old man."

A slow smile began to work its way to the lips that were drawn back in a harsh, straight line. "Never claimed not to be." He eyed his nephew, knowing he had him. "Do we have a deal?"

Henry held out his hand, waiting for Lukas to take it.

Lukas slid his hand into his uncle's grip, trying not to notice that it felt far weaker than it usually did. It made him acutely aware of Henry's mortality.

"We have a deal." He rose from the gurney, signaling to a nurse. "All right, let's see about getting you healthy enough to live to be ninety-nine."

Henry looked at him indignantly. "One hundred," he corrected.

Lukas laughed. "One hundred," he agreed.

Chapter 10

Elliot stood in the middle of the cavernous loft that held little else than sunlight. This was where the anonymous phone call had sent them hurrying to—an empty loft above an abandoned warehouse in the rundown factory section of Norwalk. Traffic had been a bear, due to all the construction on the 405 freeway. It had taken them twice as long as it should have to get here, apparently all for nothing.

Frustrated, Elliot shook his head, the gun he'd held drawn and ready when they'd entered the deserted loft still in his hand.

"Well, if they were here, they certainly aren't anymore. Maybe it was a bogus tip."

The surge of adrenaline that had shot through Lydia when they'd forced open the door had yet to settle down. It felt as if someone was playing cat and mouse with them. She hated being the mouse.

Lydia scanned the room, squinting against the sunlight. Stooping, she ran her fingers along the floor. "It wasn't bogus. They were here all right."

Curious to see what she'd found, Elliot crossed to her. But unless her vision was a hell of a lot better than his, there was nothing in front of her except scuffed floor. "What makes you so sure?"

She held up her hand. There was no telltale dirt. "When did you ever see a loft this clean?" Rising, she brushed one hand against the other out of habit rather than need. "They cleaned out everything before they took off." She frowned, moving around the empty loft. There was nothing left behind except one sagging sofa, an obvious holdover from the last real tenants. "Tell you one thing, I'd like to hire these characters to do my place."

As Elliot watched, Lydia crossed to the dilapidated sofa and began flipping over the cushions one by one.

Holstering his weapon, he joined her. "What are you doing?"

She tossed the second cushion onto the floor, after the first. "When I was a kid, whenever my parents had people over, this was how I got my spare change after everyone else left the room. Found a wallet this way once. Maybe one of our supremacists left something behind they didn't count on leaving."

It was worth a shot, though it was a long one. But right now, other than a comatose suspect who might or might not come around, they had nothing else to go on. "Anything?"

Tossing the last cushion aside, she took out a handkerchief as she bent to pick up something amid the dirt and stale crumbs of some unidentifiable meal trapped beneath one of the cushions.

"Two dimes and a nickel. And this." Using the handkerchief, Lydia held up a small detonation cap for his inspection. "They were here."

He nodded. They'd gotten lucky after all. "I'll call the crime lab boys, have them dust the whole place." Elliot laughed dryly under his breath. "They ought to love that."

"Probably not, but it's their job. And it's 'techs,'" she corrected.

Phone in hand, ready to call, Elliot stopped to look at her. "What?"

"They're 'crime lab techs,' not 'crime lab boys.' They've got a woman on the team now. Holly Shapiro," she told him, though she doubted it would stick. Elliot had a real problem when it came to remembering names. Faces he never forgot, but names escaped him on a regular basis. "She wouldn't take kindly to being left out."

"Techs," Elliot repeated with an obliging nod of his head as he pressed a series of numbers on the keypad. Contacting the people he was after, he gave them the necessary information and location before ringing off. He flipped the phone shut, then pocketed it. "By the way, where were you this morning?"

Lydia looked out the huge multipaned window. Here the dust had been left undisturbed, acting as a natural curtain to the activities that had to have gone on inside. Was this where it all had begun? The meetings, the hate that was encouraged and urged to feed on itself? It looked not unlike any other loft in any other industrial area. But it wasn't.

Absently she realized that Elliot had asked her a question and was waiting for some kind of an answer. "My cell was off."

"The lab bo—techs'll be here in half an hour, barring any traffic jams," he told her. "You weren't at your place, either," he added casually.

Lydia raised an eyebrow as she looked at Elliot, the questions finally registering. "Checking up on me, Elliot?"

He spread his hands wide, an overly innocent expression on his rounded face. "No, just glad you're getting a life, that's all."

Janice had been talking to him again, Lydia thought with an inward sigh. Why did married people always think you weren't happy unless you were spoken for, too? "I have a life, Elliot. With the FBI, investigating crazies who get carried away with incendiary devices."

He ignored the warning note in her voice. "Can't keep you warm at night."

Very carefully, she placed the detonator cap into a fresh plastic bag she had in her pocket. "That's why God invented electric blankets, Elliot."

He watched her seal the bag. Just as she wanted to seal her life. With a quick, firm, final motion. "Look, I'm not prying…"

The hell he wasn't. "Good," she said dismissively.

Elliot debated withdrawing, but he liked Lydia too much to perpetually respect her privacy at the expense of telling her what she needed to hear for her own good.

Moving around so that he was in front of her as she began to head out of the loft, he said, "But just for the record, I think maybe you should admit to yourself that your dad wasn't perfect."

Lydia stopped dead. The look she gave him made him do the same. She did *not* want to listen to anyone, not even Elliot, analyze her behavior for any reason. "Where's this coming from, Elliot?"

"From the heart," he told her with only a hint of hesitation. Lydia exploding was a fearsome thing to witness and she exploded when people pried into her private life. But this had to be said. For her own good. "I've been your partner since the beginning. I know all about your dad, the medals, the decorations for bravery. You thought he was perfect."

She didn't like being placed in a position where she had to defend her father, but if it came down to that, she could. "He damn near was."

"To a fourteen-year-old girl," Elliot stressed. That was how old she'd been when her father was killed. Elliot was losing her and he knew it. He sped up. "My point is that maybe thinking that way is stopping you from finding someone of your own. Your mother found someone.'' If the widow could, so could the daughter, he was sure of it. ''Your stepfather's a great guy.''

They'd all gotten together for the last Fourth of July barbecue. Her mother and Arthur, Elliot, his wife and kids. And her. Was that where this was coming from? Because she'd come alone to the barbecue? Well, she'd rather be alone than tied for eternity to someone she didn't want to be tied to, simply to avoid being lonely, which she was not.

She also couldn't picture spending the rest of her life with someone like Arthur, kind though he was. Arthur could put fireflies to sleep.

But because her mother had lived on the edge for all those years, worried that the next time the phone would ring it would be someone to tell her bad news about her husband, Lydia could readily understand why Louise had married Arthur.

''Yes, he is,'' she readily agreed. ''He's just not my father.''

She'd be the last to admit it, but Elliot knew there was hero worship involved in the way Lydia felt about her father. The man had died too soon for her to discover the flaws he had, the ones everyone had that made them human.

''No man will live up to your father, Lyd, until you take him off that pedestal.''

Elliot was her best friend as well as her partner, but she could feel her patience wearing thin. ''Can we talk about something else now? Like about what they're paying us to do?''

He nodded, knowing that it was time to retreat. ''I've said my piece.''

She pinned him with a look, warning him that he'd better stick to his word. ''Good.''

Because he was her friend, Elliot couldn't help adding a coda. ''For now.''

Lydia groaned as she preceded him out of the deserted loft.

Lydia got off the crowded elevator on the fifth floor at Blair Memorial and automatically scanned both sides of the corridor. She wasn't just looking around for anyone suspicious, she was also keeping an eye out for Lukas.

She wasn't at all sure just how she would react the next time she encountered the good doctor after what had happened between them last night, but she knew that an encounter was inevitable. With Elliot going to the office to run down some information regarding the detonator cap she'd discovered, Lydia had elected to return to the hospital to check on Conroy. With the frustration of a near fruitless morning behind her, she wanted something positive to happen. More than anything, she wanted Conroy awake for questioning.

She walked into the glass-partitioned room, nodding at Rodriguez, and found that there was no change in Conroy's status. He was still unconscious, still in the coma he had been medically eased into for his own well-being.

She studied the man's face. He looked dead to the world. Her patience felt as if it was on a short lease. Turning away, she looked at the special agent she'd left watching over the prisoner. "Dr. Graywolf show up this morning?"

Rodriguez tucked away the magazine he'd been perusing. She noted that the cover boldly announced the current football season. "Early."

"And?"

The wide shoulders that had once belonged to a promising college fullback rose and fell. "And then he left."

She blew out an angry breath. "Did he say anything?"

Looking properly intimidated, Rodriguez shook his head. "Not to me."

"Great. Where is he now?" Ethan opened his mouth to reply, but she anticipated his negative answer. "Never mind, I'll have him paged. Just continue doing what you were doing."

Pushing the door open, she left the room.

Nerves were adding to her agitation. Nerves that were dancing like beads of water dropped on a sizzling-hot pan. Why, damn it?

Was it because they'd slept together?

Her mouth curved despite her mood. It was an entire misnomer. Very little sleeping had gone on last night. But even so, it wasn't like her to have any qualms about interacting with someone she'd slept with. It hadn't happened often, but it had happened, and she hadn't been uncomfortable with the situation.

This time, though, it was different. This time she wasn't remotely comfortable with the situation. She would like to blame this state of unrest on Elliot and his pep talk, but she was too good an investigator for that. The nerves had been there before Elliot had ever opened his mouth in the loft. They had sprung up early this morning, the moment she'd opened her eyes and intensified when she'd discovered she couldn't make good her silent escape.

She didn't like feeling nervous, wasn't used to it. It was like watching the sky, seeing the storm clouds gathering, and waiting for that first loud clap of thunder to shake the earth.

Try as she might, she couldn't seem to smother the feeling and make it go away.

But this was her problem, no one else's, and somehow she was going to have to deal with it.

Coming to the nurses' station, she had a nurse page Lukas, then stood back and waited to confront the source of her unrest about her prisoner. It didn't put her in the best of moods.

Lukas's office was in the medical complex directly across the street from Blair Memorial and, since it was just a little past noon, he decided to forgo making a call and to respond in person to the page.

He came fearing the worst. That the call was about

his uncle. He'd had Henry checked into the hospital and, not wanting to rely on whatever Doc Brown's office might eventually fax over, Lukas had left orders for a battery of tests to be done to determine, as accurately as possible, the exact state of his uncle's heart. He had also left strict instructions to page him at the first sign that his uncle was in any immediate danger.

Hurrying out of the elevator, his face an impassive mask to hide the turmoil going on within, Lukas quickly arrived at the nurses' station.

"What's the emergency?" he demanded of the woman behind the counter.

"I am."

Turning, he saw Lydia coming out of the alcove where that floor's coffee machine was housed. There was a paper cup in her hand.

The tension of the morning interfered with what might have been, under any other circumstances, a nice moment. If Lydia had been the one to have him summoned, the problem wasn't about his uncle. Relief hid behind annoyance at being made to rush over.

"What is it?" he asked crisply.

She didn't like his tone. It sounded edgy, bordering on anger. Did he think she'd had him paged for personal reasons? Now that their night of passion was behind them—maybe even a notch on his belt—was he afraid that there might be repercussions? That she'd want something from him, maybe even have some kind of designs on him?

The pompous jerk.

Your own fault. Lydia felt her shoulders stiffen as she cursed the lack of control she'd displayed last night.

"Conroy's still unconscious." Her tone deliberately matched his.

"I know. I checked on him this morning."

Now that he was here, Lukas decided, he would stop by his uncle's room down the hall to see if any of the test results had come back. He'd had his uncle admitted to the CCU for obvious reasons: the battery of monitors necessary to watch his condition were all here.

"Well, just how long is this going to go on?" He was being maddeningly blasé about this.

"As long as it needs to." The fine skeins of his patience unraveled. He walked to the alcove, indicating that she should follow him. He waited until she joined him. When she did, he gave it to her with both guns. "Look, Special Agent Wakefield, I have other patients to tend to. I've done all I can for Conroy. The rest is up to him. I can't come running over here like some lackey every time you want to know 'are we there yet?' like some kid on a cross-country drive. We'll be there when we're there. Do I make myself clear?"

For two cents she'd haul off and hit him. Had she been twenty years younger, she would have. But she wasn't. And she had a position to maintain, so she kept silent.

''Perfectly,'' she stormed, turning on her heel and walking away.

Angry with her for triggering his outburst, with himself for his uncalled for reaction, and with the anxiety that was gnawing away at his insides, the fear that his uncle's problem might be too serious for him to handle, Lukas silently heaped curses on his own hot head.

He started to go after her, to somehow make amends and apologize for snapping, but his pager went off again. This time it was his office.

Torn, he decided that he was in no condition to say anything to Lydia that she would remotely consider redeeming. By the look in her eyes when she turned away, she was too angry. She'd probably cut off his head if he tried to apologize right now—and with good reason.

He hurried off to answer his page.

She was bored, and her eyes had begun to droop. But the instant she heard the door open, Lydia stiffened, her body alert.

Stiffening was the last thing she needed to do. Her whole body felt as if rigor mortis was setting in. Taking over for Peterson after his shift was over, she'd been sitting beside Conroy for the past two hours in the darkening room, waiting for him to come to. Willing him to open his eyes again.

Trying not to think about what Elliot had said to her earlier about her father.

Trying not to admit that maybe there was a germ of truth in it.

Her hand on the hilt of her service weapon, she stared as she saw what looked to be a white cloth poking through the opening between the door and the frame. What the hell was going on?

Slowly the door opened and then Lukas walked in. He crumpled the cloth in his hand, tossing it aside. "They told me you were here."

"I am," she replied crisply. Angry about the dressing down he'd delivered in the corridor this afternoon, she wasn't about to give him an opening to repeat his performance. Her tone kept him several leagues away.

Well, this is awkward, he thought.

He'd had the rest of the afternoon to chastise himself for his behavior and to try to explain it to himself. The obvious reasons were only partially responsible. There were other, deeper reasons and he didn't know how to go about exploring them without undermining himself. So for now, he left it alone.

But he couldn't leave what he'd done alone. He'd always believed in owning up to his mistakes and in trying to make amends, no matter what it cost him. And this time, it was going to cost him a lot, he thought. Because absolution wasn't going to come easy.

She rose. "If you want to examine him, I'll get out of your way."

He'd never seen a look so stony, which, considering the things he'd done as a youth, was saying a lot, he thought.

Lukas caught her arm as she passed him and realized it was the injured one when she winced. He released his hold immediately. "Sorry."

"It's all right," she muttered, flexing her arm. Wanting nothing more than to leave the room. Calling herself a coward for the very desire.

She was going to leave anyway. Lukas placed himself in her path. "No, I mean I'm sorry. Sorry for this morning."

Lydia lifted her chin, defiant, her eyes almost blazing. "So am I, I should have been gone before you woke up."

She still didn't get it, he realized. "I'm talking about this morning in the hospital." This wasn't easy, but it had to be said. "I had no right to talk to you that way."

"Well, we seem to be in agreement there." She paused. "Look, you had a lot on your mind, it's all right."

He thought of his uncle. The tests had all indicated that Doc Brown knew what he was talking about. His uncle needed bypass surgery. The sooner the better. Not wanting to wait, he'd scheduled it for eleven the next day, giving his uncle enough time to prepare mentally. Lukas would have rather done the surgery immediately, but it wasn't an all-out emergency and he hadn't wanted to alarm the old man. A calm state of mind could only help Henry.

He squelched a sudden desire to touch her face. It had all but blind-sided him.

"You're right. I did have a lot on my mind, but it's no excuse to take it out on you."

"Fine, you made your apology," she said coolly. "Now examine your patient and then leave so I can go on doing what I'm here to do. My job," she emphasized.

He saw beneath the cool tone. Saw because she employed the same defenses he did. He'd hurt her, he realized. And it was going to take more than a crisp apology to make amends.

"I'm not here to examine the patient. I'm here to apologize and you're not making it easy."

Her eyes scrutinized his, looking for the truth. "I don't make anything easy."

"So I'm learning." He glanced at the overhead clock on the wall. "When do you go off duty?"

She'd brought a copy of the notes on the case with her to read tonight. "I wasn't planning to tonight."

He saw the thick file on the table. Probably her reading material. "Then take a break. I'd like to talk to you in private. Get someone to cover for you." He nodded at the unconscious patient. "This is a baby-sitting detail anyway."

She frowned, looking at him for a long moment. "All right, I'll give you twenty minutes."

"Twenty minutes is fine." He knew he wanted a lot more than twenty minutes. But for the time being, he'd settle for that. At least it was a start.

Chapter 11

She peered into the open area outside Conroy's room and called to Rodriguez. The special agent was busy talking to a young, fresh-faced nurse and making nice progress from the looks of it, Lydia observed.

Rodriguez was at her side instantly, eager to be pressed into service.

She knew she was going to disappoint him. "Stay with the prisoner for a few minutes for me, will you?"

"You got it, Special Agent Wakefield."

She had to keep from smiling. The man made "special agent" sound as though it were a noble title, second only to "queen." "Thanks." Lydia walked outside, through the double doors to the inner corridor that separated the CCU area from the rest of the hospital.

Once there, she had second thoughts about going anywhere with Lukas. He could say what needed to be said here in the corridor. She turned abruptly toward him. "Look, there's no need to apologize, privately or otherwise."

Her voice was distant, detached, but he saw the fire in her eyes. Fire that pulled at him, hypnotically pulling him closer.

"I think there is," he told her quietly. "At least I'd like to explain why I jumped all over you like that earlier."

She felt her back going up. If he was trying to salve his conscience, he wasn't about to get away with it with a few well-chosen words. "You don't have to, I know why."

"You know?"

Just how extensive was her intelligence monitoring? Were the examining rooms bugged now? He knew that was technically against the law because of doctor-patient privilege, but he wasn't naive. There were ways to get around almost anything, openly or covertly.

"Sure I know." Did he think she was born yesterday? "You're afraid that I want to make something of last night."

He suddenly began to realize why she'd reacted the way she had. "And you don't?"

No. Yes. Maybe. The retorts all jumped out at her. She had no real answer to that, but she had only one response she was willing to give him: no.

Seeing someone come through the electronic doors toward the CCU, she moved to the other side of the hall and lowered her voice.

"We're both adults here, both capable of enjoying ourselves, of having a good time without attaching any meaning to whatever happens. You obviously thought when I had you paged this afternoon that I just wanted to see you again or to ask when we could get together." As she spoke, the ice in her voice dissolved, fueled by the heat of her barely suppressed anger. "Or something equally juvenile and clingy, using Conroy as a convenient excuse. And just as obviously, you don't know me very well. That's not my style."

Though it made no sense, there was something stirring about seeing her angry. When she finished, he crossed his arms in front of his chest, studying her. Amused for the first time that day. "Pretty sure of yourself, aren't you?"

She didn't like the superior attitude he'd assumed. Lydia wasn't about to back away until she put this smug bastard in his place. "I'm generally right."

"And have you ever been juvenile and clingy?"

"I already told you that isn't my style." Her eyes narrowed into glittering green slits. "Not a damn single time."

He hadn't thought so. "Gives us something else in common—along with matching chips on our shoulders." The curve of his mouth faded into a straight, stoic line. "Except the man who taught me how to get rid of mine walked into the hospital this morning looking for me. For my help.''

She swallowed the impulse to deny the comparison, to crisply tell him that any chips he thought he saw were fabrications of his imagination, but there was something in his voice that made denial secondary to curiosity. Whoever had come looking for him was someone he felt something for.

''Heart trouble?''

Lukas nodded. His eyes said things to her that his lips hadn't. He was talking about someone who mattered. A great deal. Someone who caused him to leave behind his stoic mask.

This was going to take longer than the twenty minutes she had promised him. Lydia set aside her own wounded pride and took out her cell phone. When he looked at her curiously, she held up her hand to hold back his questions.

''Give me a minute.'' Within seconds of pressing the familiar number, she was talking to Elliot. She turned her back on Lukas, lowering her voice. ''Elliot, I hate asking, but I need you to come down and stay with Conroy.''

''You mean in addition to you?''

''No.'' It took a great deal for her to ask for a favor, even of Elliot, but right now the man she had allowed into her world for the briefest of interludes needed someone and though she wasn't entirely sure why she was doing this, she had elected herself to that position. "I know I said I'd take the first baby-sitting shift but—" She bit her lip. "Trade shifts with me."

There was a pause on the other end. Just when she was about to ask if he had heard her, Elliot responded. "Sure."

She thought she heard Janice in the background, asking him what was wrong. Guilt nibbled away at her. "I wouldn't ask—"

"—if this wasn't important. I already know that, Lyd." He also knew what she was probably thinking. "Janice and I didn't have anything planned for tonight except growing a little older together. I'll be there in fifteen minutes."

"You can take longer than that. Rodriguez is on duty for another half hour." She glanced over her shoulder to where Lukas was waiting for her. "I owe you," she told her partner.

There was a soft chuckle in her ear. "I already know that, too. See you, Lyd."

She snapped down the lid on her cell phone and slid it into her pocket. Elliot would be as good as his word. With Rodriguez still on for another half an hour acting as backup and with Conroy still unconscious, there was nothing to prevent her from leaving with Lukas.

Crossing to him, she felt those same jumpy feelings skittering through her that she'd felt last night. She made a concerted effort to block them out.

"All right," she told him as he looked up at her, "we can go for that coffee now."

* * *

They elected to take his car to the small outdoor coffee shop located several blocks away. Nightfall darkened the perimeters of the landscape and the breeze rolling in from the ocean a scant mile and a half away made the evening chilly.

Sitting across from Lukas at a small table that accommodated two, Lydia wrapped her hands around her coffee cup to warm herself. For a man who had wanted to talk, he was rather silent.

She waited until the waiter who had brought them their coffees withdrew.

"So tell me about this patient who walked in this morning. Is he the one they paged you about from the hospital?"

Lukas nodded. "It's my uncle Henry."

The words felt as if they each weighed several pounds as they emerged on his tongue. Why was it so hard for him to share anything personal? People did it all the time. The airwaves abounded with people who called radio talk shows, eager to spill their insides to any stranger with five minutes to spare who was even moderately willing to listen. Here was a woman with whom he had shared the most intimate of acts, and he was hanging back, reticent to say a single word that smacked even remotely of something private.

She waited for him to continue. When he didn't, she coaxed softly, "Tell me about him."

"You mean his condition?" He'd reviewed the

tests again just before coming to see her to assure himself that waiting until tomorrow wasn't a mistake. He had a margin, but the surgery had to be performed tomorrow to remain on the safe side of that margin.

"That, too." But she was far more interested in his relationship with his uncle. Far more interested, she realized, in finding out things that she hadn't uncovered in her cursory background check. "You had this look in your eyes when you referred to him in the hospital…" She let her voice trail off.

He remembered referring to Henry only as a patient, not as a relative. "I didn't say his name."

"You didn't have to." Cold, she took a long sip of her coffee and let it slide down her throat. She set the cup down as she studied his face. He had an incredible profile, she thought. Something she would have expected to see in a bronze sculpture by Remington. "The Young Warrior" it would have been called, she decided. "I could tell there was some kind of connection between you two even before you said a word. Did he raise you?"

"How did you know—" And then he stopped as he remembered. "Oh, I forgot. You did a profile on me, or ran an APB or whatever it is you call it when you special agents dig things up on people."

She didn't take offense at the crisp shift in tone. He was throwing up a smoke screen, most likely to protect something vulnerable.

"You make it sound sleazy," she said mildly. "I just wanted to know who I'm dealing with."

Lukas relented. There was no call for him to have said that. That was the private him reacting. But he'd been the one to invite her here, not the other way around, he reminded himself.

"I suppose that's fair. I just don't like people prying."

He had the vague feeling that he was repeating himself. But his mind wasn't on his words. It was on the woman in front of him. The one who had turned to liquid fire in his arms last night. The woman who, despite his best efforts to place this all in perspective and at a distance, made him want to repeat everything he'd done last night—and double it.

Damn it, he should be thinking about the surgery tomorrow, not about making love with her tonight. Especially since the latter wasn't going to happen.

"So tell me about Uncle Henry."

Toying with the remainder of his coffee, he raised his eyes to her. "What don't you know?"

"Pretend I don't know anything." She took another sip, then looked at him. "Start from the beginning."

The beginning. Had there been a beginning? Looking back now, it felt as if Henry had always been part of his life. But, of course, he hadn't.

"He's my mother's older brother. Henry Spotted Owl. She asked him to move in with us about a year after my father died. Told him I was too much for her to handle and that she was..." His voice trailed off as the right words didn't come.

"Afraid you'd come to no good?" Lydia guessed.

He laughed shortly. That was the cleaned-up version, he supposed. "Something like that. I ran with a gang on the reservation. They believed in the old philosophy of might makes right." As he spoke, it almost felt as if he was talking about someone else. Had he really been that wild young kid or had that all just been part of a bad dream?

Her voice, soft, low, brought him back. "Did you get in trouble with the law?"

He shrugged carelessly. "Just minor scrapes." But they had been on their way to major ones. "Until the joyriding incident."

"Joyriding incident?" she prodded. His juvenile records were sealed, but she'd had her suspicions about what was in them.

He nodded. In his mind's eye, he could see it all again. His friends, the white Mustang they'd all crammed into. The exhilaration of speed as they had careened around corners, heading toward oblivion.

But there was no reason to go into that. Or into the fact that for the first time in his life, driving around at almost one hundred miles an hour, he'd felt free. He gave her the short version.

"I didn't know the car was stolen. Got my behind thrown into the local jail. My mother called for Henry." He laughed. "That was the first time I saw him. Big, old, ugly man, with a scar running down his cheek. Three inches." He held his thumb and index finger apart to underscore the length. It had made

Henry seem that much more menacing. "Said it was knife fight that made him find his way. Called it his Badge of Courage." It saved him from dying in some alley, Henry had added. "Anyway, he came to the jail, bailed me out and took me back to my mother.

"The whole ride back he said nothing." Lukas remembered almost going crazy with the silence. "Just let my imagination run away with me." He drained the remainder of his coffee and set the cup down on the saucer. "I figured once I got home, he'd pound me into the ground the way my father used to. But he didn't." That had been his first surprise.

"What he did do was tell me that from now on, I was going to tow the line. First thing he did was get me to work at the gym he established on the reservation." Lukas had found out later that because of him, his uncle had closed down the gym he'd been running in a neighboring town and brought all his resources to open the one on the reservation. "I was there every morning before school started, sweeping the place out, getting equipment ready for the day ahead. After school he had me training to be a boxer."

She looked at him in surprise. That hadn't been in the background report. "You box?"

There'd been competitions, prizes. He shrugged. "I can hold my own. Won second place in a tournament a couple of times." The prizes weren't important now, but they had been then. He'd wanted to win. And to make Henry proud of him. "He straightened me out, said that boxing saved his life and maybe it could do something for mine." It was a simple approach, but effective. "He was right. I had a punching bag to work out my frustrations on instead of thumbing my nose at the world and seeing how far I could push everybody."

Lukas turned up his collar against the breeze that was becoming colder. She looked unfazed by it, he thought, her face a picture of rapt attention. He wanted to lean over and kiss her.

"I love that old man. And he never asked anything from me." He paused and sighed. "Until this morning."

She could feel his tension, guess what he was feeling. "Can you help him?"

He had done the procedure enough times. But never on someone he cared so deeply about. "The hospital and I'd rather someone else do it."

"And he'd rather you do it." It wasn't a guess.

"Yeah." It was more than just a matter of preference. "He's never cared much for doctors. I can't remember his ever going to one. The only time he was inside a hospital was to take me to the emergency room when I was on the wrong end of a right hook. Caught me completely unaware. I went down hard, cutting open my head." It had scared the hell out of him. A split second before his head had hit the canvas, he'd thought he was dead.

Lukas lifted his hair and she saw a small, angry

scar just above his ear. She resisted the urge to trace it with her fingertips.

"There was blood everywhere. Uncle Henry drove his old pickup like it was a race car at the Indianapolis 500." All he'd been aware of was the pain. And jostling from side to side as his uncle drove. "Did the thirty miles to the closest hospital in about twelve minutes." Lukas laughed softly. "Only time I ever saw him look scared." He sighed, looking at Lydia. "He won't let me recommend anyone."

Lydia put himself in the older man's position. "Why should he? He wants the best."

Did she have any idea how heavy a burden that was? "What makes you think I'm the best?"

A smile slid slowly over her lips. "Research, remember?"

"Yeah, well, this time I might not be the best." The possibility of what might happen was already haunting him. "What if I slip—"

His self-doubt surprised her. And made him human in her eyes. It also gave them something in common. She wasn't the only one who had self-doubts in the wee hours of the night.

"You won't," she said with more confidence than he felt. "And the important thing is, he trusts you. I'd say it's a lucky thing that your specialty allows you to help someone you love. Stop resisting and be glad he came to you. The alternative," she added, "is a hell of a lot grimmer."

He let out a deep sigh. "You're right, it is."

She took a last sip of her coffee and made a face. It was cold. She pushed the cup away. "So when's his surgery scheduled?"

"Tomorrow at eleven. Triple bypass." How many times had he written that into a chart without a qualm? But now it was his uncle who was going to go under his knife. Henry, who he loved far more than he had ever loved the man fate had made his father.

Lukas had a lot on his mind. No wonder he'd exploded. She'd done it herself with far less crowding her thoughts. "I'm sorry I got in your face about Conroy this morning."

Her apology struck a raw chord, making him feel guilty again.

"You were just doing your job. I'm the one who should be sorry. I'm supposed to be able to control my emotions better than I did."

His apology made her laugh. He looked at her quizzically for an explanation.

"Sounds like we're both a couple of sorry cases." She felt him slip his hand over hers. This time, rather than stiffen, she held her breath. Waiting. Hoping. Slowly, she raised her eyes to his.

"Come home with me, Lydia."

She felt her heart accelerating. "You don't say my name very often."

"Kind of hard to spill your guts to someone you call 'Special Agent.'" He paused, aware that he was

In Graywolf's Hands

tense, that he was needy even if he didn't want to admit it to himself. "So, will you?"

Lydia was already rising to her feet. "You didn't have to ask."

Silence and small talk filled the interior of Lukas's sedan as he drove her back to the hospital parking lot where she'd left her car.

From there, Lydia followed his vehicle to Lukas's apartment, all the while wondering if she had the slightest idea what she was doing.

What she was doing was getting personally involved, which was against every rule she had ever laid out for herself. Granted, it wasn't as if Lukas was related to her prisoner, but if not for Conroy—more to the point, if not for the shot she'd fired at Conroy, she would have never met Lukas.

And that, she realized, would have been a waste. A waste no matter how this was all destined to end— tonight, tomorrow or a week from tonight. That she was in a finite situation she never questioned. What she questioned was whether or not it would ultimately affect her judgment and her performance on the job.

She told herself it wouldn't. That she was thinking as clearly as ever.

And what she thought—clearly—was that what was happening here was too intense for her not to explore, not to sample. Yes, she was happy with her life, yes she was glad she was an FBI special agent, but being with Lukas made her aware that she needed

more than work. It made her aware that there was
another Lydia Wakefield, one who occasionally did
need the touch of a man's hand along her face. A
Lydia who had needs that had not been addressed in
a very long time. Hell, she thought, even cacti needed
to be watered once in a while to continue growing.

And this was her watering.

Still, she felt unsure as she brought her car to a halt
in the guest parking area adjacent to the carport where
Lukas parked his own car.

Maybe this was a mistake. Maybe she should just
start her car up again and go home to devote herself
to going over the case tonight. To get her mind back
on her work and not on how a man who moved like
a proud god could bring every one of her five senses
alive.

She wasn't opening her car door, Lukas realized as
he got out of his sedan. She'd slipped into a desig-
nated parking space before he'd pulled into his, but
she hadn't made a move since then.

Was she having second thoughts? He'd had them
himself as he'd led the way to his apartment complex,
glancing every so often into the rearview mirror to
make sure she was still following him. Each time he
saw her, there'd been a sense of relief he couldn't
readily ignore.

His second thoughts had melted away the instant
he'd begun to replay the moments they'd shared together last night. Moments that made him want her
with an intensity that he found unnerving.

Biology was something he was aware of every day, but not on this level. This was something else, something special. This, he only now began to see, made him feel alive.

Not just alive, but real. He couldn't put it in any better terms for himself than that. It's was if he'd been moving through a world filled with shadows for most of his life and had just now wandered into an area that was filled with light.

Light and substance.

And an FBI special agent.

He wondered if it was a coincidence that her last name had the word "wake" in it. Because things were waking up within him.

He was probably making too much of it, he told himself.

And then again, maybe not.

Lukas walked over to where Lydia had parked her car. The driver's door was open, but she was still sitting in her seat, apparently undecided whether she was coming or going. Looking at her, Lukas put out his hand and waited.

After a beat, Lydia placed her hand in his and got out of the car.

Chapter 12

Leaving his keys on the small side table by the front door, Lukas turned on the radio. Soft, bluesy music filled the air.

The music made Lydia feel like swaying. Like kissing him, she thought, turning to look at Lukas. Slowly, she slipped off her jacket and then her holster, draping both over the back of the armchair.

Anticipation rippled through her, finding a resting place within her inner core.

"You seem tense," she noted, moving closer to him. The scent of his cologne, fading now, stirred her nonetheless. Exciting her. "Is it tomorrow's surgery, or me?"

"Both." Lukas held his hands out in front of him. There wasn't so much as a twitch in any of the muscles. But inside? That was where the nerves were doing their thing. Unsettling him. Making him doubt his own abilities.

As if reading his mind, she brushed her hand along his cheek. Suddenly she wanted nothing more than to comfort him.

"Don't spend time doubting yourself and second-guessing tomorrow. You're doing a disservice to both yourself and your uncle."

He didn't take flattery well, she thought. Funny how much they had in common when she thought about it. Glowing words never sat well with her, either. But she sensed that despite this trait, he needed encouragement. Because tomorrow's surgery was different.

"And he needs you to be as good as you were with Conroy." That was the irony of it. He probably hadn't even stopped to think before operating on the prisoner. And no one would have wept if Conroy had died. There was no family, nobody except the other members of his group, all of whom had apparently scattered. "Surely if you can operate on scum like that and bring him back from the dead—twice—" she reminded him "—you can perform the same miracle for someone who deserves it."

That was just it, Lukas thought. When you operated on the heart, it always seemed to involve a miracle or two. But he shrugged, falling back on the oath he'd taken upon graduating. The oath he believed in. "Everyone deserves to be helped."

"Some more than others," she emphasized. Frowning, she tried to block out thoughts of the man she'd left Elliot guarding. She didn't want to waste any time on Conroy tonight. She wanted to carve out a small island, a haven, for herself—and for Lukas— just one more time. "Don't get me started."

He smiled at her, his eyes holding hers. Stirring her up. Again. "I was under the impression that you already were."

Lydia found that her breath was beginning to catch, just as it had last night. It made talking difficult. "That depends on which way you want the evening to go."

"I know my preferences."

Moving her hair back from her neck, Lukas pressed his lips against the sweet slope. He heard her gasp and felt a thrill pass over him.

Her eyes fluttered shut as the sweet sensation proceeded to light a match to everything in its path. This time, because she knew what was coming, because she knew the magnitude of what was about to happen between them and within her, her anticipation was twice as intense, twice as electric.

Swallowing the moan that was struggling for freedom, Lydia laced her fingers together behind Lukas's head and brought his mouth down to hers. Kissing him for all she was worth.

His fingers were already undoing the buttons on her blouse, working them loose swiftly. Beneath them, he could feel the pounding of her heart. As it echoed the beat of his.

Damn, but she excited him. Worried as he was, concerned as he had been all day, just by being with him like this she managed to wipe almost everything from his mind.

Everything except her.

He wanted her so badly he could taste it, feel it in every fiber of his throbbing body. What kind of black magic was this, to ensnare him so? To make his blood rush with a fierceness that he'd never experienced before?

He'd always been able to detach himself from a situation, to view it from a lofty perspective. It was what kept him free, independent. His own person.

But he was too enmeshed here to be able to place any distance between himself and what was happening.

Nor did he want to.

Though it wrested control away from him, Lukas dearly wanted to be immersed in this, wanted to feel and taste and breathe nothing but her.

This, he knew, was nothing short of madness. And he didn't care.

It was as if he'd stepped into another world. One made up entirely of emotions. After a lifetime of holding his own in check, no matter what, to feel this way was liberating.

Hunger beat at him with both fists, urging him on.

He came close to ripping her blouse from her body when the last button refused to leave its hole.

Lukas whispered a curse. The outline of the word rippled against her mouth.

Lydia moved her hands beneath his and undid the restrained button. Her lips never left his.

Everything felt as if it were transpiring in a swirling haze that was traveling in a circle through her brain. It was hard for her to think.

It was as before. Except more so.

"Think this time we'll make it to the bedroom?" His question formed waves of warmth against her mouth.

"We can try," she murmured.

It made no difference to her whether they wound up making love in a bed, on the kitchen table or the floor. All that mattered was that they did.

Trembling, she undid the buttons on his shirt and peeled the material away from his chest, yanking it down his arms. The instant her fingertips touched his skin, something shivered through her. She sucked her breath in sharply, as if she'd touched a flame.

Maybe she had.

Each taste of his mouth, each pass of her hand along his skin, only fueled her appetite.

More warm shivers passed over her as Lukas unhooked the clasp at her back. When he eased her bra from her breasts, her body tightened in anticipation. She bit her lower lip, her fingers weaving through his hair, pressing him close as he bought his mouth down to her soft peaks, suckling at each until they became hard.

Moistening her with desires that threatened to explode within her if he didn't hurry.

She'd never wanted anyone like this before. Afraid, she shelved fear to the back of her mind as she raced toward the climax that waited for her only a hairbreadth out of reach.

Divesting Lukas of his jeans and briefs, she surprised him by pushing him to the floor, then straddling him. Smiling at the look of amused surprise on his face, Lydia threaded her fingers through his on either side of his body. Bringing her body tantalizingly down to his.

Moving so as to bring his excitement almost to fruition, she rained small, fleeting butterfly kisses along his upper torso. She could feel his desire ripening beneath her. Unable to check her delight, she laughed with pleasure as she raised her head to look at him.

"Damn, but you are some kind of a witch," he murmured fondly and in awe.

Pushing his hands into her hair, he framed her face and brought her mouth up to his. The kiss deepened and intensified, swallowing them both.

Unable to hold back any longer, Lukas arched and drove himself into her. He felt her stifled yelp of pleasure and approval.

The ride was hard, swift, and rocked them both. He heard her cry his name against his ear before he sought out her mouth again. Pleasure drenched him, mingling with the sweat of his body and hers.

Slowly he felt the tension leave her body as she relaxed against his. The afterglow embraced them both in loving, warm arms, holding tight. Lukas smiled, not trying to figure out any of it.

She could feel his smile forming against her cheek. Still dazed, she raised her head to look at him. His lower lip looked slightly swollen. She realized she must have bitten it. "What?"

"We still haven't made it to the bed." The bedroom seemed a million miles away. And he was growing rather fond of the floor in his living room.

She sighed, her breath tickling his chest. Rousing him. "Maybe next time."

He lifted her hair, then watched as it fell back down like golden rain. "You're giving me an awful lot of credit."

Lacing her fingers together, she rested her hands on his chest and leaned her chin against them, looking into his eyes.

"Just calling it as I see it." She blew softly, watching his skin tighten in response. Glorying in the response. "Feel relaxed yet?"

He laughed, his chest rising and falling, making her move, as well. Lukas stroked her head fondly.

"If I were any more relaxed, they could serve me up as a liquid compound." He wanted her again. Was this normal? Or had she cast some kind of spell over him? "Is this something they taught you in special agent school?"

Lydia moved her head slowly from side to side, the ends of her hair tickling his skin. Arousing him when he'd been certain beyond any doubt that all he had the energy for was to fall asleep.

"This is something that just seemed to happen." She realized that she was smiling and that she felt happy, really happy. She couldn't remember the last time she'd felt like this. "Maybe you bring out the best in me as well as the worst."

Folding his arms around her, he held her close against him, ensuring that she couldn't get up quickly. "What would you say if I told you that I felt like bringing out the best in you again?"

The smile grew as her eyes began to shine. "I'd say you were incredible."

"Right back at you," he murmured. He brushed his lips against hers once, twice, then pulled his head back again. His eyes searched her face, looking for an answer before he asked his question. "Stay the night?"

He was asking her this time rather than taking his chances on it happening because she'd fallen asleep. She pressed her lips together, knowing that the right thing wasn't, at bottom, what she wanted to do.

"I shouldn't."

He heard the hesitation in her voice and felt victory within his grasp.

"We'll put it to a vote." Bringing her hand up to

his lips, Lukas turned it over, palm side up and pressed his mouth against the soft flesh. His tongue lightly flicked the center. He saw desire blooming in her eyes and felt her wriggle against him, sending salvos of fresh desire through him. "I vote yes."

She swallowed, knowing the battle was lost. Lost because she had no desire to fight it. Still, she couldn't go without firing at least a shot in protest. "You're not playing fair."

"Never said I would. I'm rigging the vote," he told her simply.

His tongue swept along her palm, then her wrist. He watched as her eyes closed again.

Delicious sensations hammered their way through her body. Creating riptides of pleasure.

"Oh, what the hell," she laughed, moving up against him, bringing her mouth down to his.

"My sentiments exactly," he told her before there was no more time for talk. Only actions. Only sensations.

And for feelings that were subtly, covertly being unwrapped.

The sound of his even breathing seeped into her consciousness, rousing Lydia from what had been a light sleep at best.

Opening her eyes, she found herself staring at the ceiling. Neither one of them had had the energy to make it to the bed, although Lukas had gallantly offered to carry her. She'd turned him down, knowing he was as exhausted as she was.

He'd fallen asleep within moments of her refusal, proving her right. She'd drifted off herself minutes later.

Now, sleep dissolved like morning mist burned away by a rising sun. She lay beside Lukas, his arm draped protectively over her again, and listened to him breathe. Idly wondering what it would be like to wake up to that sound every morning.

Wondering what it would be like to have someone in her life on a permanent basis.

Whoa, where was this coming from?

Startled, completely awake now, Lydia wrestled with the feeling of well-being that still had its arms wrapped around her. What was the matter with her? There was nothing to wonder about. Nothing permanent to contemplate. She knew that this feeling was only temporary, was already fading away.

To believe otherwise would be to play the part of a fool, and she'd never been that.

There was no place for this to go. Oh, there might be a few more wild, exhilarating couplings ahead for them—maybe—but there was nothing beyond that.

Couldn't be anything beyond that, she insisted silently, forcing herself to turn away from him and to look back up at the ceiling. She already had a significant other. The FBI.

There was no room for any other relationship in her life.

Not that she expected this—whatever *this* was—to even remotely approach the realm of a relationship. It was, as the song went, "Just One of Those Things." Nothing more.

She couldn't let it be anything more. For her own sake. And for his.

Lukas wasn't sure what had wakened him. There was a time when he had been a light sleeper, but in general, when he slept now, he slept soundly, deeply, until his body told him it was time to get up. This time a sound, a feeling, roused him.

For a second, as he opened his eyes, Lukas felt disoriented. A dark foreboding hovered over him, but he couldn't put a name to it.

And then he remembered. He was operating on his uncle today. Consciousness came to him with a vengeance.

Looking around, he saw her. Last night came flooding back to him. Last night and the night before.

But there was no time to dwell on either of the feelings that occupied the battlefield of his mind.

Lydia was fully dressed, he realized. Fully dressed and, by the way she was moving around, apparently trying to leave the apartment without waking him.

Why?

He propped himself up on his elbow. "Is this part of your covert training?" She swung around, a startled expression on her face, to look at him. "Leaving the scene of the crime before the other party has a chance to come to?''

Lydia raised her chin. He was beginning to recognize her defensive movements.

''I wasn't aware that there was a crime.''

''Maybe that was the wrong word,'' Lukas allowed. It bothered him more than he wanted to acknowledge that he'd caught Lydia trying to slip away. He could understand it the first time, but not the second. ''I'm not exactly at my best first thing in the morning.''

''Neither am I.''

Sitting up, he regarded her for a long moment. ''So maybe we'd better not say anything that either one of might regret.''

Lydia looked at him, weighing her words. Looking for a way out. She had thought she'd come to terms with things yesterday just before she'd entered his apartment, but apparently she hadn't. She didn't know why it was there, but she was aware of a hint of panic pinching her.

''There's nothing to regret.'' She tried to keep her voice casual. ''We made love.''

His eyes pinned her, not letting her just shrug off last night and the night before. ''Several times.''

''Several times,'' Lydia echoed. She took a breath. ''And it was good.''

He raised a brow, wondering if he was being cavalierly dismissed, after all. His pride rebelled. ''Just good?''

She licked her bottom lip. There was no earthly reason why she should be feeling nervous. These things went on all the time. With no consequences.

"Very good," she allowed. "But not anything that's about to change either one of our lives." She squared her shoulders, daring him to disagree. "I think we're both agreed on that."

He wasn't sure why she was saying what she was saying. But he knew that he wasn't about to argue with her. Not when she was so adamant about downplaying what had been, quite possibly, the best night of his life.

Lukas had felt something last night, really felt something. Somewhere in the middle of their lovemaking, things had changed for him, making him sit up and take stock. Since there was no alcohol involved, he knew that what he'd experienced was rooted in feelings. Making love with her had only made him want to continue.

Not only that, but later, when the roller coaster ride had stopped and he'd lain there, holding her in his arms, the afterglow had been strong, gripping. So much so that he wanted to be able to experience it again.

And again.

It was out of character for him.

And then Lukas realized what she was doing. Why she was protesting so loudly that last night had just been good sex and nothing else. It *had* been something else for her. She *had* felt something and feeling it was out of character for her, too.

She'd felt something just as he had and maybe it scared the hell out of her just the way it did him.

They were both independent, headstrong people and from what he could ascertain, they were both used to being in control and on their own. He wasn't in control here. Whatever had gone on last night had controlled him. Had made him a prisoner just as much as the man in the hospital who was handcuffed to his bed was a prisoner.

Maybe it had made a prisoner of her, too, and that was what she was fighting so hard again.

"Are you sure we're both agreed to that?" he finally asked her.

"Yes," she snapped, then her tone softened just a little. "At least, I'm sure."

As long as she denied that anything of substance had happened between them or existed between them, he couldn't go any further. Pride wouldn't allow it.

"Well, then there's nothing more to talk about, is there?"

A sadness washed over her even as she expected to feel a flare of triumph. The flare didn't come.

"No," she agreed evenly. "I guess there isn't." She hesitated. "Except that I hope your uncle's surgery goes well."

Reaching for his jeans, he tugged them on before getting up. Maybe it was time he got his mind off passion and onto the business of living. And saving his uncle's life.

"Thanks." On his feet, he closed the snap on his jeans. "It will."

His voice was distant. Just as she wanted it to be. She had no idea where this sudden wave of frustration and annoyance that surged through her was coming from.

"I'd better go," she told him, beginning to back away from Lukas.

She was reaching for her pager when it went off. As did his.

Chapter 13

"Say again?"

Suddenly feeling numb, Lydia covered her left ear as she listened intently to the voice on the other end of her cell phone. Hoping that she'd somehow misheard. Rodriguez had been the one to page her. When she'd returned his call, he'd come on the phone almost breathless and extremely agitated, although he was doing his best to control himself.

He took a deep breath now. "Two of Conroy's men disguised themselves as orderlies and managed to slip past the guards."

She tried to read between the lines, anxious to get to the point of the young special agent's call. "They took Conroy?"

"No." In his haste to tell her everything, he was

getting ahead of himself. "They're still here. One of the orderlies they stole the uniforms from managed to stagger into the hall and alert security before passing out. The other orderly is dead." His young voice was grim. "When they couldn't escape, Conroy and his people barricaded themselves in the coronary care unit. They're holding the other patients there hostage."

"Do we know who they are?"

"We played back the surveillance tapes on the fifth floor. Crime lab lifted some partial prints. Their names are Marlon Fiske, age twenty-one, and Bobby Johnson, age forty-three."

"Known felons?"

"No, that's the strange part. They're both clean as a whistle."

She didn't understand. "Then how do we have their prints on file?"

"You're not going to believe this. Fiske is a federal employee at the courthouse and Johnson's with an aerospace company that works on the space station."

She'd completely forgotten about federal employees being fingerprinted. Lydia shut her eyes, running her hand over her forehead, massaging a headache in the making. "Terrific. Just what we need. Educated racial supremacists."

Rodriguez broke with protocol and described the scene as he saw it. "All hell's broken loose here, Special Agent."

Out of the corner of her eye, she saw Lukas's

shoulders stiffen as he responded to his own page. At any other time, idle curiosity would have made her wonder what was up. But right now, there was only one thing on her mind.

"What about Elliot?" She needed to know.

There was silence on the other end of the line. Lydia felt a tightness in her chest. She refused to allow herself to think the worst. "What about Elliot?" she repeated, each word underscored.

"They took him hostage." She heard Rodriguez swallowing. "He's wounded."

"How?" she demanded.

"He tried to stop them and Johnson shot him."

She pressed her lips together, grateful for small things. At least Elliot wasn't dead. They still had a chance to get him out of there alive.

"I'll be right there," she promised, not waiting for Rodriguez to say anything further.

Flipping the cell phone closed, Lydia shoved it into the pocket of her jacket. She was already wearing her holster and service revolver.

Damn it, why had she allowed her hormones to seduce her into asking Elliot to trade with her? Why hadn't she been thinking with her head rather than with her other parts? She should have stayed at her post.

Guilt ran riot through her. It was her fault Elliot was in there now in God only knew what condition. If Conroy's men were willing to kill innocent orderlies without compunction, just for their uniforms, what would they do with the patients, with Elliot, once they really became desperate?

She couldn't let herself think about it. It would only paralyze her.

Steeling herself for what was ahead, she turned around. And saw Lukas. His face was a mask of stone. Instantly, Lydia knew he had to have gotten the same message that she had when he'd called the hospital in response to his page.

But she didn't have time to discuss it. Every second counted. Every second could be Elliot's last. She had to get down to the hospital.

"I have to go," she told him as she hurried by him toward the door.

"They've taken my uncle hostage."

Lydia stopped dead. Guilt ridden about Elliot, she had completely forgotten that his uncle was also in the coronary care unit. Damn, this was just getting worse and worse.

She paused to squeeze his arm. "We'll do everything we can to get him out safely."

He wasn't naive. Promises weren't enough. He knew how these things could go. And even if things could be resolved eventually, Henry didn't have "eventually." Henry needed surgery in a matter of hours, not "eventually."

Grabbing his jacket, Lukas was right behind her. "I'm going with you."

Lydia knew how he had to feel, but he was a civilian and the more civilians around, the more things could go wrong. This was a time when even professionals got in each other's way.

She tried to reason with him. "There's nothing you can do, Lukas. This is a matter for professionals."

His eyes darkened, riveting her in place. "Like the professionals who let them take patients hostage in the first place?"

Lydia blew out a breath. She couldn't argue with him, couldn't waste the time or find the heart. She knew that in his place, nothing in the world would have kept her on the sidelines.

She turned on her heel and threw open his door. "C'mon, I'll drive."

He fell into place beside her.

For once, Special Agent Rodriguez hadn't exaggerated. If anything, he'd understated the scenario unfolding Blair Memorial Hospital.

The smell of panic, vehicle exhaust and excitement mingled in the air, growing stronger the closer they came to the sprawling compound that encompassed the hospital. Word had already leaked out to the media. News vans and trucks from all the local stations filled the area. Negotiation through early morning traffic had gone from difficult to almost impossible.

For as many reasons as there were vehicles, everyone wanted to be at the heart of what was going on.

Frustrated, Lydia maneuvered her car in as close as possible and left it double parked beside a Channel 12 news van.

"If they want to get out, they're going to have to run over my car," she declared testily as she got out.

There was a sea of people everywhere she looked. In the distance, she saw a dark van opening up and members of a swat team begin to emerge. Reporters making love to the camera as they recited their piece could be seen scattered throughout.

"It's a damn circus," she stormed, angry that tragedy was so marketable. "Don't these people have some meaningless award shows to cover or a celebrity to hound to death?"

Lukas heard the anxiety in her voice. He'd overheard part of her conversation earlier, enough to know that her partner was one of the people who'd been taken hostage. He didn't have to ask to know that she was blaming herself. He would have done the same in her place.

"Looks like for this morning, the supremacists are the celebrities," he told her.

The throng, comprised of reporters, camera personnel, curious onlookers and, more than likely, some family members of the hostages, was thickening to the point that getting through was almost impossible. Lukas saw Lydia elbowing someone out of the way, only to be confronted with another human wall.

"Get behind me," Lukas instructed. Not waiting for her to comply, he stepped around Lydia so that his body was in front of hers. Taking her hand, he forced his way through the crowd, growling a terse,

"Get out of the way," to anyone who didn't immediately move as he forged a path for the two of them.

The police stopped them just in front of the front doors. A man who looked as if he were a twenty-year veteran of the force blocked their entrance.

"You can't go in there."

Lydia took out her badge, holding it up to the man's face. "FBI. That's my prisoner upstairs."

"Right now," the policeman said, backing away, "your prisoner has prisoners."

"Dr. Lukas Graywolf," Lukas identified himself, flashing his plastic hospital ID at the man. He left it around his neck. "Those are my patients being held hostage."

"Good luck to both of you." The policeman nodded them on their way, throwing himself in front of the doors the instant the crowd began to swell forward.

Reporters were firing questions at them from all angles, wanting to know everything from the names of the people being held to how something like this could have happened and how did they feel about it.

Lukas's response to that was something that would never make the air waves.

"Does this mean your job?" a woman asked, shoving her microphone at Lydia.

Lukas shoved it away as he ushered Lydia through the door. "No, but it'll mean yours if you don't get that out of her face. Now," he growled a moment before both he and Lydia disappeared into the building.

Inside, the situation was no better. Nurses, orderlies and several doctors were all milling about, amid the police who had been immediately called in once the assaulted orderlies were discovered.

Lydia sidestepped a woman who had her arms wrapped around herself and was crying. As quickly as possible, they made their way to the elevators.

"I can take care of myself," she told Lukas.

"Nobody's disputing that," he stated in the same tone she'd used.

She opened her mouth, then shut it again. No one had thought to behave like a white knight toward her for a very long time. A small part of her rather liked that. Being looked after. If that was weak of her, she figured she could be forgiven, just this once.

Her tone softened. "Didn't mean to jump all over you."

Lukas shrugged. Maybe he shouldn't have snapped, either.

"Forget it," he told her. "We're both under a lot of pressure."

And it was going to get worse, he thought, before it got better.

Though there were fewer people, the scene on the fifth floor mimicked the one on the ground floor. There seemed to be people everywhere in the hall.

Lukas saw one of the nurses he recognized standing to the side, looking stricken. There were tears stream-

ing down her face. It took him a moment to remember
that the woman's husband was an orderly at the hospital. Had he been the one who'd been wounded, or
the one who had died? His heart went out to her, but
there wasn't time to ask. There was only time to try
to save the living.

A policewoman was coming at them, waving them
back before they could get very far. "Sorry, this
floor's restricted."

Holding her badge up for the woman's benefit,
Lydia pushed passed her. She spotted Rodriguez and
made her way toward him. Agitated, worried, she was
only vaguely aware that Lukas was following in her
wake.

"How the hell could this have happened?" she demanded of Rodriguez before she was next to him.
"We had people stationed downstairs."

The younger man lifted his shoulders helplessly. "I
don't know, Special Agent Wakefield. I was just coming on when someone came up behind me, screaming
that people had been killed and that the terrorists were
barricaded in the CCU."

"'People'?" she demanded. "Be specific. How
many dead?"

Rodriguez tried to compose himself. His inexperi-
ence shimmered in his voice. "So far, we only know
about the orderly."

Facts, she needed facts. "You said Elliot was hurt.
How do you know if you weren't here?"

"One of the nurses on the floor saw him go down

when the two orderlies—I mean, terrorists, stormed the corridor in front of the CCU. They dragged him inside with them as the doors closed.''

To be used as a bargaining chip. She fought back the angry tears that had sprung to her eyes. Tears weren't going to help Elliot.

"How do you know he's not—how do you know he's just wounded?" Rodriguez said nothing. He didn't know the answers to her questions, she thought, exasperated. The realization stung. For now, to get through, she concentrated on procedure and not on what might be happening behind the barricaded doors. "Did you notify the assistant director?"

"He's on his way down with more manpower. And I called Special Agent Peterson's wife."

Thunderstruck, her eyes widened. "You did what?"

The demand echoed loudly enough to momentarily evoke silence around her as everyone turned toward her and the young special agent.

"I—I called Special Agent Peterson's wife," he repeated, fearfully this time.

"Why in God's name would you do a thing like that? I don't want her here, going through hell—"

"Lydia?"

It was too late. Janice, a small, earthy-looking woman, was hurrying toward her, her face a pale, drawn mask of terror. Behind her, the elevator was just beginning to close.

The policewoman stepped toward her, but Lydia

waved the uniformed woman away. "It's all right, she's with me."

"Lydia, is it true?" Janice cried. "Is Elliot in there?"

"Yes." Crossing to the older woman, she embraced her as Janice began to cry. Lydia took a moment to try to comfort her, then motioned a nurse over. "Take care of her," she instructed. "We'll get him out, Janice. I swear to you we will."

Janice could only nod bravely as she pressed her lips together to keep the sobs from emerging.

Lydia turned back to doing what she did best, analyzing the situation. There was no question in her mind that the supremacists had cut the power to the electronic doors that separated the CCU from the rest of the hospital. Otherwise, they would have opened the moment she'd stepped into the sensor's path.

The chair where Rodriguez had sat last night was unoccupied. His desk was devoid of the file box and the visitor registry book that had been on it earlier. The only thing that remained in place was a telephone.

She looked at Rodriguez. "Does the phone still work? We need to be able to communicate with those bastards."

The novice dragged his hand nervously through his dark hair. "I—I don't know."

Raising her voice, she asked, "Anyone know the number?" as she looked around.

Lukas came up behind her, reciting the seven digits that would connect her to the telephone.

"Hold it." Lydia took out her cell phone. "Okay, again." She punched in the numbers he repeated.

A second later, the phone on the desk behind the barricaded glass doors began to ring. It rang a total of twelve times before she saw the doors on the right wall just beyond the desk opening.

At first it looked as if no one was coming out, and then she became aware of movement along the floor. Whoever had come out was snaking his way to the desk like a guerrilla soldier out of a grade-B movie.

Shifting from foot to foot, she waited impatiently for him to pick up the telephone. The second she heard a voice on the other end, she began talking.

It didn't surprise Lukas that the first words out of Lydia's mouth were a demand. "Let me talk to Agent Peterson."

Lukas could almost make out the man's expression. He was scowling and looked as if he'd just started to shave on a semi-regular basis. "Who?"

Was he playing dumb? Lydia wondered irritably. "Peterson. Elliot Peterson. The FBI agent you have in there with you."

It was obvious that the man didn't care for the tone she was using. "Look, lady, you're in no position to make any demands."

She wanted nothing more than to get her hands around the man's neck.

"There's a SWAT team getting off the elevator,"

she told him. "And a combined force of a hundred guns pointed in your direction from all angles. I'd say you're the one who's not in a position to make demands."

The information didn't rattle the man behind the barricade. On the contrary, it seemed to infuse him with more bravado.

"We can kill everyone here before you can get to us," he bragged.

Terrific, she was dealing with someone whose mind had never made it beyond an elementary school playground. "I'm not about to get into a spitting contest with you. Let me talk to Agent Peterson and then you tell me what you want for Christmas."

He looked up. For a second, despite the distance, their eyes locked. "Sorry, he can't come to the phone right now."

The defiant tone unnerved her. "Why?" she demanded. An answer came to her. *Oh God, please don't let him be dead.*

Lukas saw the look on her face, heard the glimmer of fear in her voice an instant before she valiantly banked it down. There were other patients in there, not just his uncle, and since he was the only doctor who was this close to the scene, that made them his responsibility.

Without asking, he tilted Lydia's cell phone so that he could hear what the other man was saying, as well.

Understanding Lukas's reasons, she didn't even look at him quizzically.

The baby-faced supremacist, whom she assumed had to be Marlon, didn't bother to answer her question. Instead, he made his first demand. "We need a doctor in here. Conroy, he's not doing too well."

She could give a damn about Conroy. "How badly is Agent Peterson hurt?"

The voice on the other end snorted. "We'll let you know once we get that doctor."

It wasn't going to go like that. If she let Fiske get the upper hand in the bargaining, everything would be lost. "You don't get a doctor—you don't get anything—until I see Peterson. Is that clear?" Behind her, she heard Janice sobbing.

"Doctor first," the young man snapped. "It's not negotiable."

Lukas placed his hand over the bottom of the cell phone. "I'll go," he told her.

But Lydia shook her head, vetoing the idea. She had enough to worry about without thinking of him being in there, as well.

"We'll get someone else," she told him. Placing the cell to her ear again, she returned to negotiations. "Okay, how's this? I'll trade you a special agent for a special agent."

The pause on the other end was ripe with confusion. "No. He stays here."

She had to get Elliot out. Nothing was going to go forward until she saw her partner safely away from the supremacists. She wouldn't allow it.

"Look," she began tersely. "If he dies, he's not

going to do you any good and killing a federal agent is punishable by death, I don't have to tell you that. No fancy lawyer is going to be able to get you off. He dies, you die. That's the law and it's written in stone. Now, what'll it be?''

There was a pause on the other end of the line and then Fiske told her, ''I've got to talk this over with the others. What's your number?''

She gave it to him. The line went dead.

With a sigh, Lydia snapped the cell phone closed. ''He's going to talk it over.'' She spat the words out. Frustration clawed at her.

''You can't be serious.'' Lukas's tone rebuked her. She raised her eyes to his, not catching his drift at first. ''You can't go in there.''

It was her job to go in, to bring about peace at a decent price. Did he think she was just playing at law enforcement?

''You are.''

He waved away the comparison as just so much nonsense. ''That's different. I'm a doctor. There are people in there who need medical attention.''

If there was a difference, she didn't see it. ''And one of them's my partner. Who wouldn't be in there if I hadn't suddenly decided to trade with him.'' She worked her words past the lump in her throat. ''Well, I owe him a trade. He said so last night. This is it.'' She looked at Lukas. ''This isn't negotiable, Doctor. He's in there because of me.''

Lukas understood that, understood her guilt. But

not her recklessness in proposing to change places
with the other man.

"I can treat Elliot—"

Lydia looked at him. Was he that naive, or did he
simply not understand that the scum beyond the barricade did not subscribe to the same noble principles
that he did?

"Conroy's too weak to make it out of here in his
present condition. Those men in there with him are
not going to let you do anything until you bring about
some kind of miracle for Conroy." She saw the impassive look on Lukas's face. She knew it frustrated
him that she wasn't listening to reason—his reason,
not hers. "I don't answer to you, Lukas. This is something I need to do. We need someone on the inside
and that someone is me."

Rodriguez had been standing to the side, listening
to the exchange. He moved forward now. "Special
Agent Wakefield, I could go in—"

She stopped him before he got any further. "No
offense, Rodriguez, but you're still learning."

He did his best to appear as if he was on top of
things. "Best place to learn is on the inside."

He was smiling, but she detected the nervousness
just beneath the surface. Not that she blamed him.
Nerves were healthy. They kept you from doing stupid things and kept you alive.

She placed her hand on his shoulder. "I need you
out here, Ethan. You get to face the assistant director
when he comes," she reminded him. "Personally, I'd

rather face these maniac supremacists.'' The phone in her hand rang. She exchanged looks with Lukas. ''Looks like it's showtime.'' She tried one last time before flipping the phone open. ''I can't talk you out of this?''

His eyes on hers, Lukas shook his head. ''Not a chance.''

Lydia sighed. ''I didn't think so.'' She pressed the button on her telephone as she turned to face the man on the other side of the barricade. This time, he was sitting up at the desk, the phone to his ear. ''Did you come to a decision?''

''We'll trade the agent for you. As long as we get the doctor, too.''

''Smart move,'' she said, only praying that she was making one that was smarter.

Chapter 14

Back on the telephone, Marlon Fiske made his first demand.

"Send the doctor in first."

"No." Experience had taught Lydia that if Lukas went in before the trade for Elliot was made, no one would be coming out. "We need a show of good faith on your part. Send out Agent Peterson."

Fiske's face contorted. "Do you think we're stupid?"

Worried, angry at the terrorist and at herself for not being here when this had gone down, Lydia looked through the glass directly at the man. Hell, he looked no older than a college freshman. He should be lounging around in a frat house, sneaking in a beer and planning what to do on Friday night, not terrorizing coronary patients.

It was hard holding on to her temper and keeping her voice calm.

"I think you know that you're in a very precarious position. You have other hostages. I already told you that if anything happens to Agent Peterson, you won't be in a position to bargain for anything. Now send him out," she said evenly. "I'll meet you halfway. I'll take a step for every one he takes. An equal trade, like I said. And then you can have the doctor." She couldn't help adding, "That's more of a fair deal than you gave anyone at the mall."

Fiske looked at her angrily from across the barricade, his brow furrowed in indecision.

"Take it or leave it," she told him when his indecision stretched out the silence.

Lukas covered the cell phone in her hand with his own. She might have her agenda, but he had his. He couldn't risk the lives of any of the patients behind the barricade. Jacob Lindstrom, the man he'd operated on just before Conroy arrived in the E.R. had mercifully been transferred to his own room yesterday afternoon, but there were others there, others who had to be terrified by what was happening.

"I've got to go in there, whether or not he agrees to the trade." According to what a nurse had just told him, there were five patients currently in the CCU, not counting Conroy. Four were post-operative and one, his uncle, was pre-operative. All of them required close monitoring. There were hospital staff members trapped inside with them, but he couldn't count on them being able to handle an emergency situation.

Lydia looked into his eyes. She understood where he was coming from, but it didn't change anything. "We have to do it my way. You can only come in from a position of strength, otherwise, we lose them all." She saw the doubt. "I know what I'm talking about, trust me."

It all boiled down to that. Trusting her. Trusting someone else to handle things. It wasn't something he was accustomed to doing.

"What are you two whispering about?" Fiske demanded, his voice rising out of the cell phone.

She turned back to look through the glass. Fiske was peering at them uncertainly. Almost nervously, she thought. She had to use that to their advantage.

"That it's a nice day for a negotiation," she said simply. "So, what'll be?"

"Okay," he barked angrily. "Come ahead."

She placed her hand on the door. It wouldn't budge. There were chairs and a table piled against it. "You're going to have to clear off some of the debris before I can get in."

Fiske took two steps toward them, then stopped. "Back up!" he ordered, loud enough for his voice to carry through the doors. "Stand where I can see you."

"We won't rush you," Lydia promised. There was nothing to be gained if they did. The other man inside the unit could easily kill the hostages in retaliation. "You have my word."

Fiske sneered. "The word of a government pig doesn't go too far."

A smile with no humor behind it curved her mouth. "Pig senior-grade carries some weight on this side of the door, even if not on your side," she assured him, taking several steps back. "Nobody will make a move on you."

Her eyes never left Fiske as the supremacist, balancing his weapon under his arm, managed to pull back one of the barricades.

"Okay, you can come ahead."

But she made no move to go in. "First, get Agent Peterson. Equal steps, remember?"

Frustrated, Fiske backed up, not willing to leave the corridor unmanned now that one of the obstacles had been removed. He kept his gun trained on the doors until his body was level with the second set of double doors. Pushing open the door with one hand, he glanced in, then immediately looked back at the special agent he resented having to deal with.

"You, nurse, bring the wounded guy over here." Sparing only another glance, he motioned to the woman he was addressing with his weapon.

Lukas lowered his head so that only Lydia could hear him. "I don't want you to do anything stupid in there," he whispered in her ear.

She looked at him sharply. She thought of last night. Of how vulnerable she'd made herself, being with him. Who knew how disastrous a mistake that could have been if she hadn't retreated this morning?

"No more stupid than anything I'd do out here."

Lukas thought of the way she'd been with him initially. "That's not very reassuring."

His eyes swept over her. A myriad of emotions pushed their way to the fore. Everything had suddenly taken on a different cast in light of the dire situation. He realized that within moments, she would be at the mercy of men who had next to no regard for human life. And he didn't want her to be at their mercy, he wanted her to be safe.

"I mean it," he told her fiercely. "Don't get them angry."

Too late, she thought. "They were born angry, Graywolf." She paused to smile at him. "You ought to know a little about that. Here, hang on to this." She gave him her cell phone. "He might want to say something to you before you go in."

Movement beyond the glass caught her attention. Lydia sucked in her breath as she saw Elliot emerge from the communal CCU area. Leaning heavily on the young nurse who seemed to be doing more than her share to prop him up, he was taking shaky steps forward. There was blood all along his left pant leg.

Her heart constricted. "Oh, God."

Lukas turned to summon one of the people behind him. "Get a gurney and take Peterson down to E.R. the second he comes out," he ordered.

When he turned back, Lydia was opening the door.

Aware that his heart had suddenly lodged in his throat, he caught her by the arm.

Startled, she looked at him quizzically. If she was going to ask what the hell he thought he was doing, she never got the chance. Her mouth was beneath his in a kiss that tasted of concern, of fear, and of other things she didn't have time to decipher. There were too many emotions colliding within her for her to handle any more.

Releasing her, Lukas stepped back, seeing Lydia for the first time. Seeing himself, as well. It crossed his mind that they were living in an insane world where things became clear just when they were the most complicated.

"Be careful."

Nodding, Lydia pushed open the door.

"Okay," she said to Fiske, using her calmest voice. Fiske was watching her every move intently, nervously. She knew she was dealing with a volatile person who could pick any time to go off. It wasn't a comforting thought. "I'm coming toward you. Remember, a step for a step."

"Remind me one more time, bitch," the kid terrorist warned her, "and it'll be the last time you remind anyone of anything."

I'm going to get you, junior, Lukas silently vowed as he watched Lydia slowly make her way toward the other end of the corridor. *And make you eat every damn word out of that smart mouth of yours once this is over.*

When she was halfway there, Fiske's eyes suddenly widened and he snapped to attention as if he'd just been poked in the back by a cattle prod. "Hold it! Take your piece out."

"My piece?" she echoed incredulously. What was he, a veteran couch potato who spent his life watching old crime dramas? Nobody used that word anymore.

He obviously took her repetition as ridicule. "Your gun, bitch," he snarled, shifting from foot to foot. "Take your gun out of your holster and put it on the floor. Now!"

Very slowly, holding her jacket open with one hand, she carefully plucked the service revolver out from its holster with the other. Securing it, she held the gun aloft with two fingers. If she wanted to, the weapon's hilt would have been in her palm in an instant and she could have easily gotten a clear shot at the baby-faced supremacist. But there was the chance that before he went down, he could get off a shot at either Elliot or the nurse who was propping her partner up.

Either way, she couldn't risk it. She needed to get the drop on Fiske when he could do the least amount of damage. And when a shot wouldn't have his partner in the other room reacting and retaliating.

She bent and placed the gun on the floor in front of her.

"Good. Now kick it over here," he ordered. When she did as she was told, he nodded. "Get your hands back up over your head and keep walking." He saw her look toward Elliot. She wasn't taking a step. He cursed roundly, then looked at the nurse. "You, do the same with the lead weight."

Lydia gauged her steps to Elliot's until they were finally parallel to one another. Hands above her head, she spared one glance toward her partner. "I'm really sorry, Elliot."

He offered a weak smile. "Just when I thought it was safe to get off disability." His breathing was labored. The wound hurt like a son of a gun. "It's not your fault, Lyd." He pressed his lips together to lock out the pain. "Watch yourself."

The exchange, too low for Fiske to pick up, only succeeded in agitating him further.

"Hey, hey, hey, no talking. You got something to say, say it out loud so I can hear." To emphasize his point, he waved the gun first at Elliot, then Lydia.

She was almost next to him now. It wasn't easy bridling her contempt as she looked at him. "Okay if I put my hands down now?"

"No, get inside the room." His hand to her back, Fiske pushed her toward the communal area. "And you out there," he shouted into the telephone, "send in the doctor or the FBI agent dies."

Breaking communication, he slammed the receiver down into the cradle.

The moment the outer doors parted and the nurse emerged with Elliot, Lukas waved the gurney forward. Elliot's wife was beside him, grasping her husband's hand even as they laid him on the gurney.

"Get him to the O.R., now," Lukas ordered. "He's lost a lot of blood."

The resident took over. Lukas pushed open the door and stepped inside the inner corridor. Fiske was coming toward him. "I'm Dr. Lukas Graywolf."

Fiske stopped in his tracks. Small, cold, amber eyes looked him over with contempt. For one moment, Lukas was propelled back to his past, looking into the eyes of people who thought themselves superior to him.

Fiske's thin lips curled. "Damn it, you Indians are everywhere, aren't you?" He spat out the words.

Lukas wasn't about to allow himself to be rattled a by low life. He'd endured far more from better men than the one standing in front of him.

"We're all part of some minority or other," Lukas told him mildly. "Even you."

The fair complexion reddened with rage at the insinuation. "My people go way back."

Lukas merely looked at him, not stating the obvious. That his went back further. He wasn't here to antagonize the small-minded man, only to treat the patients.

Fiske used his weapon as an extension of his hand and pointed it toward the black bag Lukas was holding. "What's in there?"

Because he'd learned long ago to suffer fools and endure their stupidity, Lukas remained calm. "Medical supplies." He'd had one of the nurses put it together the second he knew he was going in.

Moving backward, the supremacist motioned him over to the desk.

"Open it."

Lukas complied. With the tip of his weapon, Fiske moved things around within the medical bag, more for a show of strength than anything else. Satisfied that everything appeared to be in order, he indicated the other doors.

"Okay, now get in there and fix Conroy."

The ludicrously simplistic command demanded some sort of response. "He's not a broken toy to be mended," Lukas told him evenly, preceding him into the large room.

A dozen beds separated by Plexiglas walls and sandwiched in between monitoring machinery were arranged in a large semicircle. There was a patient in every other one. His uncle had been put in the bed closest to Conroy's area. The nurses' station was the focal point of the unit. The hospital personnel who had been within them when the two terrorists had rushed the area were huddled by the far wall where they'd been ordered to stay. Three nurses and an orderly.

And Wanda.

Lukas saw the fear in her dark eyes. He nodded at her as reassuringly as he could. "It's going to be all right," he promised.

"Only if you and the government bitch don't mess up," the other supremacist, Bobby Johnson, warned him. A big man, he looked older than his age, with streaks of gray running through his reddish hair. "Otherwise—" Johnson turned his weapon on Lydia. He was holding on to her by her bad arm, Lukas realized. "Bang, she's dead."

Lukas looked at Lydia. She looked completely passive, as if she weren't even listening to what had just been said. Damn it, she shouldn't have to be here. None of them should.

"I thought the whole point of this was for you to get out of here with Conroy. You kill her and they'll never let you out alive," Lukas said.

"We don't need an Indian lecturing us." Fiske snickered, pleased to be the one who knew something the others didn't. "You believe it, Bobby? They sent us an Indian to treat Conroy. Surprised he doesn't have a rattle and some kind of magic dust with him to sprinkle on Conroy." He shook his head contemptuously. "These hospitals are just falling apart, letting anyone who wants to practice come in here."

She saw anger flare in Lukas's eyes and hurried to prevent a confrontation. The condescension toward Lukas galled her, but she had to pick her fights and right now, that couldn't be one of them. She needed to defuse the situation before it turned ugly.

"You wanted a doctor, you got the best. He saved your friend's life twice."

Her words made no impression on Johnson. "If you stinking FBI people hadn't shot John in the first place and let us get our point across the way we were trying to, none of this would be happening," Johnson yelled at her angrily, shaking her. Lukas saw Lydia try not to wince. "Now get him well enough for us to get out of here."

"And just how do you propose to get out of here?" Lydia asked as Lukas moved past both of them, crossing to Conroy's bed.

"How do you think?" Johnson sneered nastily, his eyes ravaging her. "We've got you for that. You get your people to get us safe passage out of here and onto a jet—"

Maybe they weren't as professional as she'd first thought. They certainly hadn't thought out a decent plan. "There's no place to land one around here," she pointed out. She'd gotten the particulars on Blair Memorial when Conroy had been admitted. "All we have is a helicopter pad on the roof."

Mention of the landing pad evoked a hoot of pleasure from Fiske. "That sounds good. I've never been on a helicopter ride," he said to the older supremacist.

Johnson looked at Fiske with contempt. There was no love lost between them. "Make the call and get one," Johnson ordered.

With all this gun waving going on, Lydia knew it was just a matter of time before one went off. She wished both men would keep their weapons still.

"I left my cell phone outside," she told Johnson, fervently wishing there had been time for her to get fitted for a wire. That way, Rodriguez and the others would have been able to hear what was happening. But Fiske had never taken his eyes off her and she hadn't wanted to risk upsetting the cart by temporarily ducking out of his range of vision.

"I hate careless women," Johnson growled.

His eyes were malevolent as they swept over her. Aerospace engineer or not, there was no doubt in Lydia's mind that the man was unbalanced. She just prayed he wouldn't go off the deep end and start shooting people before she had a change to disarm him.

Crossing to Conroy's room, Lukas passed his uncle's bed. Rather than fear, there was only concern on the older man's face. Despite the impatience of their captors, Lukas paused by Henry's bed. Lukas took his own turn with guilt. If he'd insisted on sending his uncle to another hospital, the man would be having the procedure done now, out of harm's way.

"You all right?"

Too weak to sit up, even with the help of the adjustable bed, Henry still managed to smile at his nephew.

"Don't worry, today is not a good day to die," he joked.

Lukas didn't like the color of his uncle's face. It was far too pale.

The next moment he felt Fiske prodding him with the muzzle of his weapon.

"You two can powwow later," the youngest supremacist sneered condescendingly. "You're here to fix Conroy, remember?"

All he needed was a clear shot at him with his bare

hands, Lukas thought. But Fiske was brandishing a weapon while standing too close to Henry. He couldn't afford to do anything yet for fear of Henry getting hurt.

Lukas was forced to do as he was told.

Walking into the small space allotted to Conroy, he paused to check the monitors surrounding his bed. The readings were good. Progress was slow, but that was to be expected, given the circumstances.

"Can't you give me something?" Conroy complained angrily. "It hurts like hell."

Lukas took hold of his wrist, gauging Conroy's pulse. "You were shot and you had heart surgery, you're lucky to be feeling anything."

Unable to remain still for more than a few seconds, Johnson was pacing at the foot of Conroy's bed. "Just fix him so he can travel, medicine man."

He knew that, to buy some time, Lydia wanted to perpetuate the ruse that they were going to be given everything they wanted, but he felt he had to give them the truth about Conroy's condition. The man had still been unconscious as of last night. His being awake was sapping all of his energy for the time being.

Lukas avoided looking at Lydia, knowing her reaction to what he was about to say. "You move him, you do it at your own risk."

Johnson hit the black bag with the muzzle of his weapon. "There's gotta be something in that bag of yours, medicine man, to do the trick. Maybe you just need some incentive. Maybe,'' his voice grew harder, ''if we start eliminating the people in the room, you can see your way clear to doing what I tell you. How about it, medicine man? Who goes first? The old lady—'' He swung his weapon toward Wanda, who looked back at him defiantly. Lukas mentally took off his hat to her. ''Or maybe your pal, here?''

As he said it, he aimed his gun at Henry. Lukas could feel the muscle in his jaw grow rigid. If they hurt Henry in any way, he was going to kill them with his bare hands.

''Better yet, how about her?'' This time Johnson aimed the gun at Lydia. ''They can only kill me once and they've already made up their minds to do it because of that kid who died at the mall.''

''Worthless punk,'' Conroy gasped. ''Served him right for coming out to see the exhibit. What the hell's wrong with people, coming out to gape at some useless scribbling and calling it a tribute. Tribute, huh. A tribute to dirty, marauding scum.'' Angry, red-rimmed eyes turned on Lydia. He nodded at Lukas. ''You know his kind killed my daughter? Killed Sally? Gave her all sorts of garbage to mess with her head. I found her in the bathroom. My daughter, dead in a pool of vomit on the bathroom floor.'' He fairly shrieked the words. ''They're all worthless, drug-snorting, foul-mouth lowlifes. I wish I'd gotten more of them.'' His eyes narrowed. ''Next time.''

''There's not going to be a next time if you go joyriding on a helicopter,'' Lukas told him.

"I'm touched by your concern," Conroy sneered.
"Just give me something to kill the pain and have the
government pig get the helicopter," he ordered.
"Otherwise, we're going to have ourselves an old-
fashioned massacre here." He looked at Lukas with
hatred as Lukas took out a syringe and a vial of mor-
phine. "You know all about that word, don't you?"

Lydia had heard just about all she could stand. "I
think you could have been forgiven if your scalpel
had slipped during his operation," she told Lukas.

"Gimme a gun," he ordered Fiske. The latter
handed him Lydia's own weapon. Conroy's lips
curled at the sheer irony of it. He'd use her own gun
on her. There was justice for you. Weak, his anger
strengthened him. "Say your prayers, FBI bitch,
we've got ourselves enough hostages, I'm taking you
out. An eye for an eye, right? You shot me, I'm shooting you."

With that, he raised the gun and aimed it at Lydia.

Chapter 15

Lukas didn't remember thinking, he merely reacted. He jabbed the needle into Conroy's arm. Jerking, Conroy screamed in surprise and pain. His shot went wild.

Lukas doubled up his fist and swung at Conroy's jaw, knocking him out.

The distraction was all Lydia needed. She swung around and kneed Fiske, who was standing behind her, frozen in place, gaping at what had just transpired. As he doubled up in pain, howling and cursing at her, she grabbed Fiske's gun away from him and spun around to find Johnson, the gun cocked and ready in her hand.

The moment she turned, she saw Johnson backing up, the gun he was holding trained directly at her head.

Triumph shone in his dark eyes.

"Drop the gun," he ordered.

Lydia caught her breath, frustrated beyond words. But the gun remained in her hand, aimed at him.

"Maybe you should follow your own advice," Lukas told him.

Johnson spared a look to the side. He was staring down the muzzle of the weapon Lukas had taken from Conroy. Rather than exhibiting any fear, the supremacist's lips peeled back in an evil smile. He was clearly enjoying himself.

"What we have here is a what they used to call a Mexican standoff."

"Wrong," Lukas contradicted evenly, not a single muscle giving away the very real concerns he had. Even if it didn't manage to get Lydia, or him, a stray shot could hit any one of the patients or the staff. He had to get Johnson to drop his weapon. "A Mexican standoff is when there's a balance of power. In case you forgot how to count, it's two to one here. Not in your favor."

"You can't kill both of us, Johnson," Lydia told him, her gun still raised.

The wild look in his eyes intensified as he swung the muzzle of his weapon from Lydia to Lukas and then back again. He cocked the gun. "No, but I sure as hell can kill one of you."

His choice of victim evident, Johnson squeezed the trigger before he finished his words. But the shot went wild, passing through the ceiling as he fell to the floor, dead. His eyes were wide, glazed and unseeing as they stared at Lukas.

Lydia stared, dumbfounded. Lukas had fired his gun before she could even squeeze her weapon's trigger. Training that had been rigorously drummed into her had held her back until the last possible moment.

And that last possible second would have been too late. If it hadn't been for Lukas.

Rounding the bed, Lukas was beside her the next moment, his eyes taking swift inventory of all her parts. "You all right?"

Numbed, she nodded.

"Everybody else okay?" he asked, tossing the question to the room. A murmur of uneven, shaky voices answered in the affirmative.

Crossing to Johnson, Lydia dropped to her knees over his body, feeling for his pulse more out of obligation than expectation. She wasn't surprised not to find any.

But she was surprised by what had just happened. She looked at Lukas, kneeling beside her. "Where did you learn to shoot like that?"

He sat back on his heels. There would be no life-and-death battles waged over Johnson. That fight was over. "The reservation. Billy Standing Bear could get his hands on almost any weapon you could think of."

His life in the wild band he had run with in his youth had included experiences about which he'd told no one, not even Henry, although he figured his uncle had had his suspicions. It was funny how things worked out sometimes. If he hadn't been part of the gang, he wouldn't have known his way around weapons and wouldn't be looking down at a dead man now. And Lydia, in all likelihood, would have been the one on the floor in his place.

Satisfied that Johnson no longer posed a threat, Lydia swung around to check on Fiske. He was still on the floor, writhing in pain. She looked at him with contempt. "We need something to tie up the junior terrorist with before he slithers away on us."

Lukas had a roll of white adhesive tape in his hand. "Way ahead of you." Crouching, he went to work.

Lydia hurried to the door to call in the others and to call off the SWAT team. She glanced over her shoulder and saw that Lukas had Fiske's hands and feet pulled together behind him.

He felt her looking at him. Lukas commented. "Not unlike tying a calf in a rodeo."

She shook her head. The man had hidden talents. "Someday, you're going to have to tell me about that childhood of yours."

Someday. The word shimmered between them as he watched her hurry into the corridor. He took it as a promise, not a slip of the tongue.

"Dr. Graywolf, I think you'd better get over here."

Wanda's voice brought him around. He didn't like the tone he heard. He tested the integrity of the tape he'd just wound around Fiske's hands and feet. Satisfied that Fiske wasn't going anywhere in the near future, Lukas rose. Only then did he realize that Wanda was standing next to a bed.

His uncle's bed.

Adrenaline shot through him like a flare. Rushing over, he felt Henry's neck in an effort to deny what he saw on the monitor. The screen was flat-lining.

"Crash cart. Get me a crash cart!" Lukas shouted, beginning manual CPR. Panic ate away at him the way it hadn't when he'd faced down Johnson an eternity ago. "C'mon, old man, we've been through worse things than this. This was just a little noise, a lot of shouting. It's over. Don't die on me now."

Counting in his mind, Lukas administered one round of CPR before the nurse came running back with the crash cart.

At the same moment, Lydia returned with Special Agent Rodriguez following behind her like a shadow. Keeping up was the assistant director and several other FBI agents who entered the room in their wake.

"He's all yours." She indicated the hog-tied Fiske on the floor, then nodded toward Johnson. Blood was pooling around his upper torso. "And you'll need a body bag for that one. Conroy was strong enough to hold up a gun, so I think he can be transferred to the medical ward in the county jail."

The assistant director looked down at the unconscious prisoner. "What the hell happened to him?"

"A little doctor-patient interaction," she replied, looking around for Lukas. Any other words faded as she saw Lukas standing over his uncle, charged paddles in his hands. Relief fled as something tightened in her chest. "Lukas?"

Exhaling as he silently rendered a fragment of a prayer of thanks, Lukas replaced the paddles on the cart and waved it back.

"We've got a pulse. Call down for an O.R.," he instructed a nurse beside him. "Tell them I've got a man up here who can't wait."

Closest to the wall phone, Wanda made the call to the first floor. Lukas didn't wait. Taking the safeties off the wheels, he mobilized the bed and began pushing it toward the double doors.

Not waiting to be asked, Lydia quickly took over the other side, helping to guide the bed down the corridor. Between them, the old man lay unconscious, lost to the drama he had instigated.

"Lukas, what happened?"

He hadn't even looked at her. His face was a grim mask. He was afraid that if he allowed himself the slightest bit of emotion, it would crack everything else apart, including his strength.

"He had a heart attack," he answered crisply, punching the button for the elevator. "I guess seeing a gun pointed at me was too much for him."

The service elevator car arrived almost immediately and they pushed the bed in. Lukas pressed for the ground floor. Praying. Praying to remember how to pray.

Unable to help herself, Lydia took the old man's hand in hers even though she knew he wouldn't feel it. Silently she tried to will him her strength. "Is there anything I can do to help?"

Lukas looked at her over his uncle's inert form. "Do you know how to pray?"

She hadn't prayed since her father had been shot. An ocean of prayers had turned out to be useless. Her father had still died. "I'm not sure I remember how."

"You might try remembering," he told her as the doors opened again.

Quickly, they made their way through the throngs in the corridors. Though questions followed them, people got out of their way. The emergency operating rooms were located next to the elevators at the rear of the hospital.

As they arrived at the doors of the first operating room, Lydia reached over the bed to touch Lukas's hand to get his attention. "Is there anyone I should call for him?"

He shook his head. "There's just my mother. She thinks he's off on a fishing trip." He set his mouth grimly, not wanting his thoughts to stray. "It's better that she doesn't know."

Lydia watched helplessly as Lukas disappeared through the double doors. She disagreed with his assessment of the situation, knowing that if she were his mother, she'd want to know that her only brother was on the operating table, fighting for his life. She'd want to move heaven and earth to be there.

But it was Lukas's call to make, not hers. She let

out a shaky breath. All she could do was be there for him when it was over.

Suddenly at a loss with what to do with herself, Lydia went to the lounge where family and friends were supposed to wait sedately while those they cared about were half a corridor away being operated on.

The moment she walked in, she was enveloped in an embrace. It took her a second to realize that Elliot's wife was pressing her tear-stained face against hers and hugging her for all she was worth.

"He's going to be all right, Lydia. Elliot's going to be all right." Stepping back, Janice covered her mouth with her hands, physically holding back a sob of joy. "They're admitting him overnight, just to be sure, but the doctor says he's going to be just fine. It looks like he just needs a transfusion. Nothing vital was hit." Fresh tears shimmer in her eyes. "Lydia, I can't thank you enough—"

Lydia shook her head. All she could think of was that if it hadn't been for her, Elliot wouldn't have been shot in the first place. "There's no need to."

"Oh, but there is," Janice insisted. "If you hadn't traded yourself for him, he could be—" She stopped abruptly, unable to say the horrible words.

There was no point in going over everything, assigning blame and denying it. What mattered at this moment was the end result. Elliot was going to be all right. Lydia smiled at the other woman.

"Hey, I'm in no mood to break in a new partner. I had no choice but to get him out of there." She gave the woman a quick, warm hug. "Tell Elliot I'll be up to see him later."

Watching her back away, Janice called after her. "Where are you going?"

"I've got a promise to keep." Lydia commandeered a folding chair and looked at the hospital attendant sitting behind a small desk in the corner. Eyeing her. "Okay if I take this? I'm just going into the hall with it."

Seeing the badge at Lydia's belt, the attendant reluctantly nodded.

"Just the hallway," he emphasized.

Taking the chair back with her to where she and Lukas had parted, Lydia sat beside the operating room doors to keep vigil. And to try to remember how to address a power she had turned her back on.

Rodriguez found her there a few minutes later. The look of concern he was wearing faded from his young face. "The assistant director's looking for you."

A wave of weariness washed over her. She supposed she was derelict in her duty, but she wasn't up to anything further now. Right now, she just wanted to be a woman waiting for her man.

"There's nothing left but paperwork, Special Agent. Tell him I'll get to it when I come in later."

Rodriguez was grinning. "No, what he wanted me to tell you if I found you was 'nice work.'" He laughed softly, shaking his head. "Somebody said that was a first for him."

"Actually, I think you're right." The man was far

from lavish with his praise. She smiled. "Tell him thanks."

Unwilling to leave her side just yet, Rodriguez hovered protectively. "Is there anything I can get you? Something to eat, maybe?"

The thought of food made her queasy. "Coffee would be nice."

Delighted to be of service, Rodriguez was already on his way. "You got it."

There were five empty coffee containers in various stages of crumple lined up beside the metal legs of Lydia's folding chair, one large one that Rodriguez had brought to her from the corner café and four smaller ones obtained from the vending machine down the hall. The coffee there was foul, but it was hot and black and she required little else as the minutes dragged themselves around the circumference of the hall clock, forming hours.

Her whole body felt stiff with tension. She was vaguely aware that bypass surgery took time, but how long she hadn't a clue. And she was afraid to go anywhere beyond the bathroom, which was conveniently located next to the vending machine, to ask someone for fear that she would miss Lukas when he came out.

She wanted to be there for him, to be the first person he saw no matter what the result of the surgery, good or bad.

Despite the massive doses of caffeine that were coursing through her veins, as well as the tension gnawing away at her, Lydia was beginning to feel sleepy. If she felt like this, what did Lukas feel like, she wondered, standing all this time over the body of his uncle, battling for his life?

She tried to put herself in his shoes and couldn't.

Most of all, she wanted to comfort him, to be there for him. But she was at a loss as to exactly what to do, what to say, once he came out.

And then the doors parted.

Seven hours after he'd gone in, Lukas Graywolf slowly walked out of the operating room, a man who had fought the good fight and was exhausted beyond words because of it. He'd taken off his mask. It dangled around his neck.

The moment the doors opened, Lydia was on her feet, almost sending her folding chair crashing to the floor. She caught it just in time, her eyes never leaving Lukas's face.

He looked pale, she thought, and she couldn't read his expression. Was he just tired, or heartsick? Had he won, or lost?

Lydia realized that despite the noise she'd made, he was oblivious to her presence. Afraid of intruding, unwilling to back away, she touched his shoulder.

"Hey," she said quietly.

He looked at her. For a second he felt as if he were still in some kind of a dream. Or was she real?

"Hey," he echoed, then scrubbed his hand over his face. God, but he felt as if he'd been in there a hundred hours. "What time is it, anyway?"

"Almost seven. An eternity since you went in." She bit her lower lip. The question had to be asked, there was no subtle way to find out the results. "How is he?" she asked softly.

"Alive." Even as he said it, Lukas was in awe of the fact. His uncle's heart had stopped and now it was beating again. The wonder of it would remain with him forever. Almost afraid to let it, he could feel joy flooding through him. "Breathing." He allowed himself a hint of a smile. "It looks good."

Relieved, she threw her arms around Lukas and hugged hard. The tears she'd held back for so many years dampened his shoulder. "I'm so glad for you."

He could feel her tears, hear her joy. Both took him by surprise. His uncle was no one to her, yet she was affected by his recovery.

"Yeah, me, too." And then he really looked at her, bits and pieces of reality floating together for him. He hadn't thought it possible, but his heart swelled even more. "What are you still doing here?"

"Waiting to find out if your uncle's all right."

Because it was a great comfort to him, Lukas slipped his arm around her shoulders, holding her close. He'd almost lost her today, too. But he hadn't. She was still alive. And here. The day had turned out to be pretty damn great. "No other reason?"

A hint of a coy smile crept to her lips. "Well, I was waiting for you, too."

He already knew that, and he hadn't been hinting

for an admission. "No, I mean it's not because of Conroy, or that other scum—"

"Fiske," she supplied. "No, they're both on their way to jail, Fiske to wait for proper arraignment and Conroy to go to the medical ward at County. A man strong enough to hold a gun doesn't have to be pampered." Suddenly she felt awkward. He looked tired and should be on his way home. She had no idea if there was a place there for her. "Elliot's going to be all right," she told him. "Janice said they were admitting him overnight for observation, but there's every indication that he'll go home tomorrow."

"That's good."

Her awkward feeling intensified. She looked at the chair. "I guess I'd better take this back to the lounge. The attendant didn't look too happy about lending it out when I took it."

But she'd taken it anyway. That sounded like her. He smiled at her. "Lydia, do you have a few minutes?"

She had eternity if he wanted it, she thought. Those few minutes this morning had changed everything for her, had made her reorder her priorities.

If she told him, he'd probably laugh at her, she thought.

"Sure." She waited. "Was there something you wanted to say?"

"Yes." He looked around. Things had gotten back to normal. It was as if there had never been a siege or a hostage situation, as if he'd just had a nightmare and now it was over. Except that she was still here. "But not in the hallway. Want some coffee?"

She laughed, glancing at the battalion of paper cups on the floor. "If you squeeze my hand, you might be able to pour yourself a cup." When he looked at her quizzically, she nodded at the mini-squadron.

"All right then, want to grab some food to go with all that coffee?" He didn't care what the pretext was, he just wanted to get her alone for a few minutes. Just long enough to get something off his chest.

Her stomach rumbled, speaking for her. Lydia laughed. "Sounds good to me."

Shedding his scrubs and leaving them in his locker, Lukas took her to the small café around the corner where Rodriguez had bought the coffee for her hours ago.

He felt edgy as he waited for their orders to be brought to the table. It was like waiting for the stage to be set, for the curtain to finally lift. The way the curtain had finally lifted for him.

He would have thought that, after all he had been through today, there wasn't an ounce of tension left within his body. Apparently, there was an endless supply.

After the second the waiter set down their sandwiches and accompanying beverages and backed away, Lukas took her hand.

"We need to talk," he prefaced, then saw her frown. "What?"

She pulled her hand back. Contact would only make what was coming that much worse.

"That never means anything good." Like an old-fashioned lawman, she headed him off at the pass. "You don't have to worry, Lukas. Just because I kept vigil while you were operating on your uncle doesn't mean I'm trying to lay squatter's rights to some space in your life. What we said this morning goes."

He vaguely remembered the words. And hated what they represented. "No it doesn't," he contradicted. "Not anymore. Things have changed."

She looked at her cola and wished for something stronger, something to temporarily settle her nerves. But that was the coward's way out. She lifted her chin, telling herself she was ready for this no matter how roundabout his path.

"What things?"

How come wrestling a gun away from a madman was easier than speaking his mind? And a hell of a lot easier than speaking his heart?

Taking a deep breath, Lukas plunged in. "You know how when you face death, your life is supposed to pass before your eyes?" She nodded. "Well, when Conroy was about to shoot you, my future passed before my eyes." He reached for her hand again. This time, looking somewhat stunned, she left it in his. "A future without you, and I realized that I didn't want it. Didn't want to go back to what I had because I didn't have anything. It had me." He couldn't say it any plainer than that, he thought. He put his entire fortune into the pot, betting all. "Now I'd like to know if you'll have me."

"Have you?" she echoed. He couldn't possibly be driving at what she thought he was driving at.

The edginess was carving neat little pieces out of him, stacking them by the roadside. "In marriage."

It was only through supreme effort that she didn't gape. "You're asking me to marry you?"

Frustration snapped its jaws around him as he feared the worst. That she'd turn him down. "I guess I wasn't making myself clear."

"No, no," she said quickly, "it's me. My brain just fogged up." Her mouth curved slightly in awe. "And I'm having a fantasy I don't want to wake up from."

She found herself suddenly wanting to share things with him. To give him a part of herself she'd held back, even when they'd made love together.

To bring them closer.

"Elliot said that my problem was that I was looking for a man like my father." She'd always denied it, but at bottom, she knew it was true. "Strong, honorable, decent to the point of being selfless."

Was this her way of gently turning him down? "Hard shoes to fill."

Her eyes reflected the smile she felt within her. "I think they've been filled. And then some."

It was his turn not to grasp what was being said. "Are you saying what I think you're saying?"

Lydia nodded. "I am if you think I'm saying yes."

The grin nearly split her face. "The answer is yes. Yes, I'll marry you. I always wanted to find a doctor I could trust." She looked at him significantly, touching her breast. "You see, I've been having some heart trouble lately."

Picking up her tone, he arched his brow. "Is it serious?"

She nodded solemnly. "Very serious."

He kept a straight face, even when he felt like cutting loose with a whoop of joy.

"Bears some looking into."

She could feel her heart accelerating with anticipation. "How soon can you start looking?"

He cupped her cheek with his hand. He was the type, he realized, who had to almost lose something before he became aware of how truly precious it was to him. "The second I get you home."

Her eyes softened, already making love to him. "Sounds good to me."

Because the tables were very small, he had no trouble leaning over the one they were sitting at. Lukas sealed his proposal and both their futures with a long, languid, deep kiss.

* * * * *

INTIMATE MOMENTS™

presents:

Romancing the Crown

With the help of their powerful allies, the royal family of Montebello is determined to find their missing heir. But the search for the beloved prince is not without danger—or passion!

Available in July 2002:
HER LORD PROTECTOR
by Eileen Wilks (IM #1160)

When Rosie Giaberti has a psychic vision about the missing prince of Montebello, she finds herself under the protection of dashing Lord Drew Harrington. But will the handsome royal keep her secrets—and her heart—safe?

*This exciting series continues throughout
the year with these fabulous titles:*

*Available only from Silhouette Intimate Moments
at your favorite retail outlet.*

Silhouette®

Where love comes alive™

Visit Silhouette at www.eHarlequin.com

SIMRC7

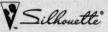

**Where royalty and romance
go hand in hand...**

The series continues in Silhouette Romance
with these unforgettable novels:

HER ROYAL HUSBAND
by Cara Colter
on sale July 2002 (SR #1600)

THE PRINCESS HAS AMNESIA!
by Patricia Thayer
on sale August 2002 (SR #1606)

SEARCHING FOR HER PRINCE
by Karen Rose Smith
on sale September 2002 (SR #1612)

And look for more Crown and Glory stories in
SILHOUETTE DESIRE starting in October 2002!

Available at your favorite retail outlet.

Where love comes alive™

#1159 LAWMAN'S REDEMPTION—Marilyn Pappano

Heartbreak Canyon

Canyon County Undersheriff Brady Marshall hadn't planned on fatherhood, but when fourteen-year-old Les came to town claiming to be his daughter, his plans changed. Alone and in danger, Les needed help and—more important—a family. And Brady needed his old flame Hallie Madison to make that happen.…

#1160 HER LORD PROTECTOR—Eileen Wilks

Romancing the Crown

Visions of a troubled woman had haunted psychic Rosalinda Giaberti's mind ever since the moment she first saw the prince of Montebello. Rosie wanted to warn him, but there were those who would stop at nothing to keep her from him. It was up to Lord Drew Harrington to protect Rosie, but could he do that without risking his own heart?

#1161 THE BLACK SHEEP'S BABY—Kathleen Creighton

Into the Heartland

When Eric Lanagan came home for Christmas with an infant daughter, his family was shocked! They didn't know about the baby's true parents or her tragic past—a past shared by her aunt, Devon O'Rourke. Eric was falling in love with Devon, and he knew that the only way to keep his daughter was to make Devon remember the childhood she'd worked so hard to forget.…

#1162 COWBOY UNDER COVER—Marilyn Tracy

Who was terrorizing the New Mexico ranch that city slicker Jeannie Wasserman had bought as a home for orphans? Undercover federal marshal Chance Salazar was sure it was the elusive *El Patrón*. Determined to catch his criminal, Chance got hired on as a cowboy and was prepared for anything—except his growing desire for Jeannie.

#1163 SWEET REVENGE—Nina Bruhns

Muse Summerfield was the hottest thing in New Orleans—until she disappeared. That was when her twin sister, Grace, and police detective Auri "Creole" Levalois began burning up Bourbon Street in an effort to find her. Creole believed that Muse held the key to his foster brother's murder, but would he and Grace survive their search?

#1164 BACHELOR IN BLUE JEANS—Lauren Nichols

High school sweethearts Kristin Chase and Zach Davis once had big dreams for their future, dreams that never came to pass. Years later, a suspicious death in their hometown brought Zach and Kristin back together. Surrounded by mystery and danger, they realized that they needed each other now more than ever.

SIMCNM0602